WHO'S COUNTING?

NANCY TAFURI

GREENWILLOW BOOKS · NEW YORK

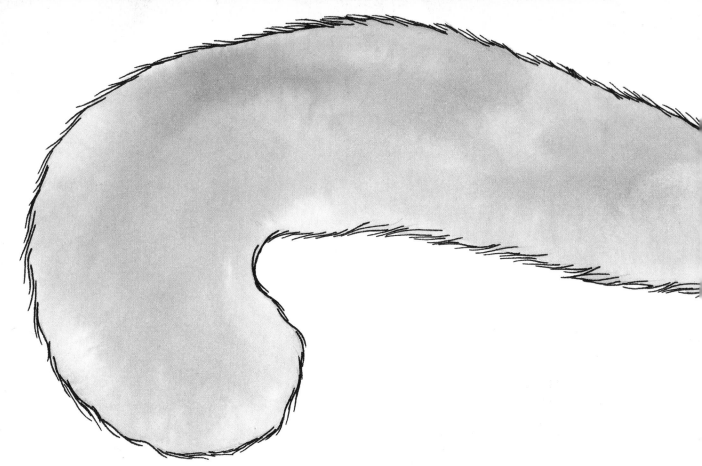

FOR ADA

A black line was combined with watercolor
paints for the full-color illustrations.
The text type is ITC Weiderman.

Copyright © 1986 by Nancy Tafuri
All rights reserved. No part of this book
may be reproduced or utilized in any form
or by any means, electronic or mechanical,
including photocopying, recording or by
any information storage and retrieval
system, without permission in writing
from the Publisher, Greenwillow Books,
a division of William Morrow & Company, Inc.,
1350 Avenue of the Americas, New York, NY 10019.
Printed in Hong Kong by South China Printing Co.
First Edition   10 9 8 7 6 5

Library of Congress Cataloging-in-Publication Data
Tafuri, Nancy.   Who's counting?
Summary: Text and illustrations of a variety of
animals introduce the numbers one through ten.
1. Counting—Juvenile literature.
[1. Counting]   I. Title.
QA113.T34 1986   513'.2 [E]   85-17702
ISBN 0-688-06130-3
ISBN 0-688-06131-1 (lib. bdg.)

1 SQUIRREL

2 BIRDS

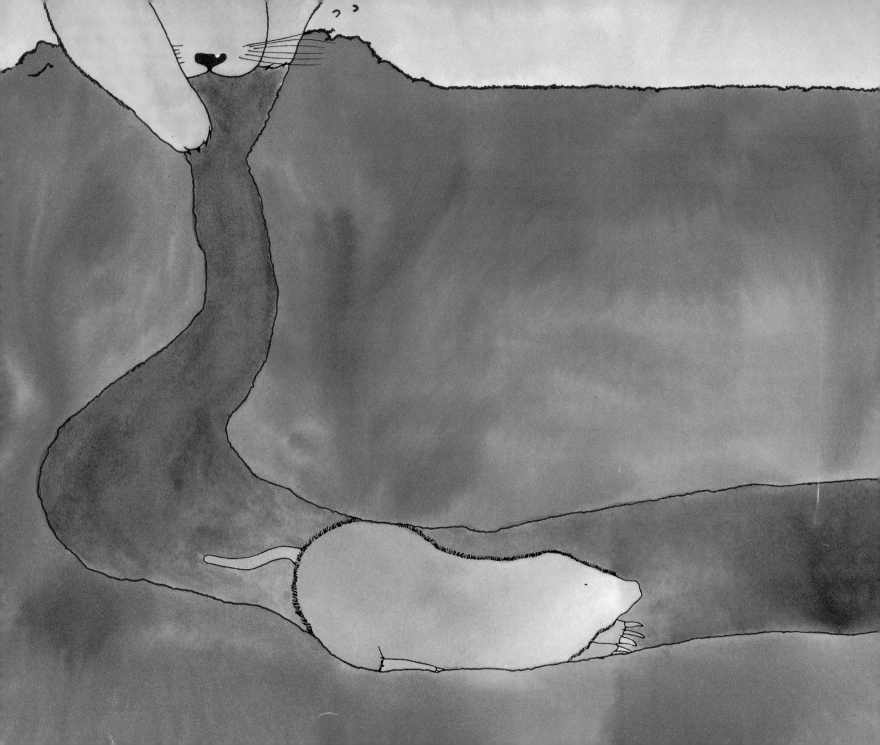

3 MOLES

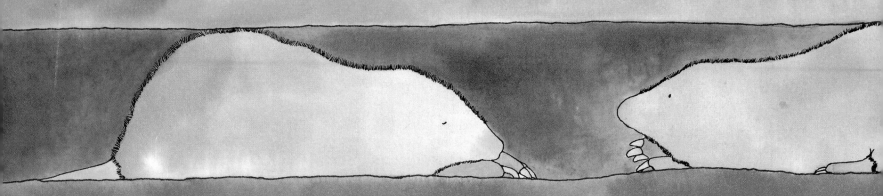

4 GEESE

5
EGGS

6 PIGLETS

7 RABBITS

8

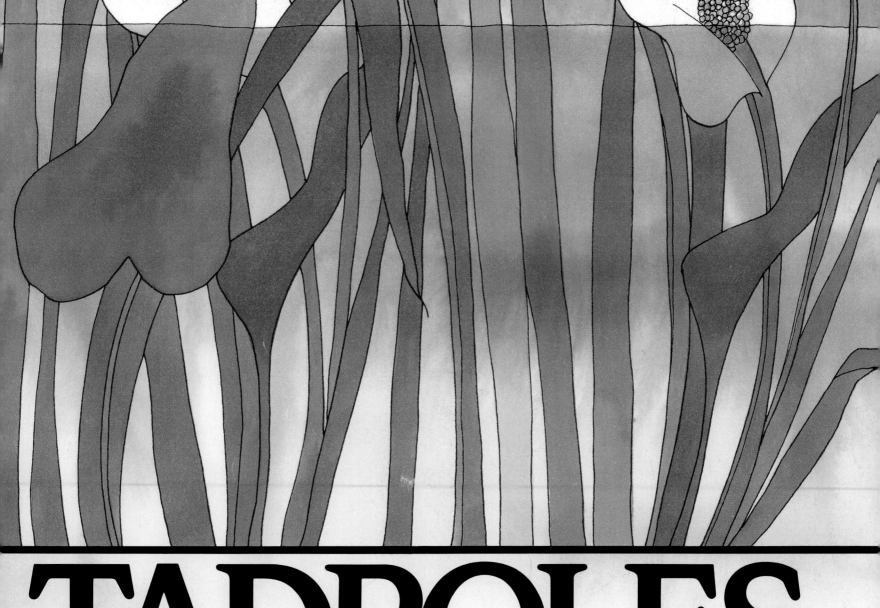

TADPOLES

9 FLOWERS

AND

10 PUPPIES-

EATING!

Permeable Interlocking Concrete Pavements

Design • Specifications • Construction • Maintenance

Fourth Edition

David R. Smith

Interlocking Concrete Pavement Institute
13921 Park Center Road, Suite 270
Herndon, VA 20171
Tel: (703) 657-6900
Fax: (703) 657-6901
E-mail: ICPI@icpi.org
Web: www.icpi.org

In Canada
P.O. Box 1150
Uxbridge, ON L9P 1N4

Every effort has been made to present accurate information. However, the recommendations herein are guidelines only and will vary according to local conditions. Professional assistance should be obtained in the design, specifications and construction with regard to a particular project.

Fourth Edition 2011

Permeable Interlocking Concrete Pavements

By David R. Smith

Fourth Edition 2011

© Copyright 2000, Interlocking Concrete Pavement Institute (ICPI).

ISBN 978-1-4507-8440-5

Published in the United States by:
Interlocking Concrete Pavement Institute
13921 Park Center Road, Suite 270
Herndon, VA 20171
Tel: (703) 657-6900
Fax: (703) 657-6901
E-mail: ICPI@icpi.org
Web: www.icpi.org

Every effort has been made to present accurate information. However, the recommendations herein are guidelines only and will vary according to local conditions. Professional assistance should be obtained in the design, specifications and construction with regard to a particular project.

Contents

continued next page

List of Figures and Tables

continued next page

Permeable Interlocking Concrete Pavements

List of Tables

Acknowledgements

Since its first edition release in 2000, this manual has evolved into its fourth edition. Each edition was informed by growing industry and user experiences as well as by academic and public agency research. This fourth edition saw much input from the Interlocking Concrete Pavement Institute (ICPI) Technical Committee and especially a task group with ICPI members Kevin Earley, chair, Rick Crooks, Brian Jones and Chuck Taylor. Thanks goes to this task group and to the committee for their time and ideas, and especially for the discussions and lively debates that resulted in best practices for permeable interlocking concrete pavement (PICP) design, specifications, construction and maintenance. The ICPI Board of Directors funded the project and without their support, there would be no fourth edition.

This edition integrates information from researchers in university, public agencies and allied industries. Major contributors to better understanding of PICP via their research deserve special thanks. These include Dr. Bill James with the University of Guelph; Eban Bean and Dr. Bill Hunt with North Carolina State University; Mike Borst with the US EPA in Edison, New Jersey; Dr. Rob Roseen with the University of New Hampshire; Dr. Derek Booth with the University of Washington; Glenn MacMillan and Tim van Seters with the Toronto (Ontario) Regional Conservation Authority. Additional support came from Kelly Collins with the Center for Watershed Protection and Tom Schueler with Chesapeake Stormwater Network, both in Maryland.

Inspiration and information came from overseas researchers including Dr. Brian Shackel with the University of New South Wales, Australia; Dr. Sönke Borgwardt, consultant, formerly with the University of Hannover, Germany; Dr. Anne Beeldens with the Belgian Road Research Agency; Dr. Stephen Coupe with Coventry University, England; and Dr. Elizabeth Fassman with the University of Auckland, New Zealand.

Allies to the industry that have influenced this edition include Glenn Herold, P.Eng., with Brown's Concrete Products, Sudbury, Ontario; Dave Hein, P.Eng., with Applied Research Associates, Toronto, Ontario; Mark Kinter with Elgin Sweeper Co., Elgin, Illinois; Harald von Langsdorff, F. von Langsdorff Licensing, Ltd. and Helga Piro with SF Concrete, both in Toronto; Neil Weinstein, P.E., with the Low Impact Development Center, Beltsville, Maryland; Bethany Eisenberg, P.E., Chair of the ASCE Technical Committee on Permeable Pavements, with VHB Consultants, Watertown, Massachusetts; and Gille Wilbanks, P.E., of WKI Engineers, Portland, Oregon, and Professor Bruce Ferguson, FALSA with the Univeristy of Georgia.

Rob Bowers, P.Eng., ICPI's Director of Engineering, assisted with drawings and detailed technical review. Deb Stover of Image Media formatted this publication.

Years ago, two persons influenced my career by providing technical and philosophical foundations long before sustainable paving and rating systems like LEED®. They are Gary E. Day, AIA, Professor Emeritus of Architecture from the State University of New York in Buffalo and Professor John Randolph at Virginia Tech in Blacksburg. They teach that the opposing forces of urban development and nature's processes can be synthesized through practical operating principles and design tools. They also teach that, given the right tools, the gap between design that respects nature and cost-effective implementation is narrower still, and that such design can effectively address social and cultural needs. Now some thirty years later, those principles are known as "sustainable design." A debt of thanks goes to Gary and John for providing me with those insights and tools, many of which are expressed in this manual.

David R. Smith
Herndon, Virginia
2011

Introduction

With about one fourth of the U.S. and Canadian population, Germany places about 10 times the amount of PICP annually. Permeable pavements are popular because the German approach to environmental protection is not only based on attenuating impacts from development. They consider the benefits of the natural environment to society. Development must regenerate, maintain and enhance it. Development must give back to nature, people and places. This notion is rooted in the German word for environment, umwelt. Its meaning embraces the health and wellbeing of people and nature. North American English would translate the German notion of a healthy environment as environmental quality. The notion transcends sustainability (i.e., meeting economic, social and environmental needs) because an implied notion is human mental or psychological health as well as environmental, economic and societal health.

The environmental impacts of impervious, monolithic pavements are well known and documented. Their erosion of human mental well-being seems to be present. It is seldom said that such pavements are beautiful. For at least a century, the blandness of monolithic pavements has certainly numbed the human mind and soul.

This manual is about deploying pavements that don't do that. It is about PICP that instead visually delights and inspires the human soul simply by looking at it, especially during or just after a rainstorm. It gives back. It does this by integrative several functions. There is of course runoff and water pollution reduction through filtering and infiltration. However, there is more. PICP reduces the urban heat island and related energy use; reduces air pollution with special cements and pigments; and reduces building energy use with ground source heat pumps. Moreover, PICP can calm traffic, be colored for way finding and blend within its broader context. Trees appreciate having it next to them and there are no puddles. This all sounds and looks like umwelt to me.

This manual is for readers who want to achieve umwelt with sustainable pavements. It takes two previously separate civil engineering fields—pavement design and hydrologic design—and integrates them. Therefore, the manual is primarily for civil engineers as well as for architects, landscape architects, urban planners and contractors. Those who use it should be familiar with stormwater management concepts and calculations such as the Rational Method and that published by the National Resources Conservation Service. They should be also familiar with the design of best management practices. The Glossary of Terms clarifies the meaning of many words and concepts used throughout the manual. Beyond the five Sections, the references cited throughout provide a wealth of information beyond this manual.

Even in its fourth edition, the manual does not portend to be complete. Industry designers, contractors and users are always learning more and ICPI is intentional about developing and improving its consensus on best practices. This manual provides criteria for selecting appropriate sites and the basics for sizing storage areas and guides selection of base/subbase thicknesses. Detailed inflow and outflow calculations can be examined using ICPI's *Permeable Design Pro* software or other stormwater models. Calculations must be done by qualified engineers familiar with hydrology and hydraulics, as well as pavement structural design using flexible pavement design concepts developed by the American Association of State Highway and Transportation Officials (AASHTO). Construction methods and guide specifications are included. Much has been learned about maintenance in the past five years and this information is included in the last Section, as well as a maintenance checklist and a model ordinance for consideration and use by municipal governments.

As readers use this manual, it should always be applied within the context of broader site designs. We trust that the outcome improves environmental quality, i.e., the mental health and well-being of people, as well as nature and the built environment. PICP does this more elegantly than any other pavement, permeable or impervious.

Section 1. Overview

Impacts from Impervious Surfaces

Urbanization brings an increasing concentration of pavements, buildings, and other impervious surfaces. They generate additional runoff and pollutants during rainstorms, causing streambank erosion, as well as degenerating lakes and polluting sources of drinking water. Increased runoff deprives ground water from being recharged, decreasing the amount of available drinking water in many communities. Figure 1-1 summarizes the impacts of impervious surfaces.

Stormwater generates intermittent discharges of pollutants into water courses. Since the pollutants in stormwater runoff are not generated by a single, identifiable point source such as a factory, but from many different and spatially separated sources within a watershed, they are called non-point sources of water pollution. During and after rainstorms, non-point sources of runoff pollution flow in huge quantities that render them untreatable by conventional wastewater treatment plants. In many cases, the receiving water cannot process the overwhelming amount of pollutants either. Therefore, the breadth of pollutants are difficult to control, as well as the extent to which they can be treated through nature's process in a lake, stream, or river.

Increased Imperviousness leads to:	RESULTING IMPACTS				
	Flooding	Habitat Loss	Erosion	Streambed alteration	Channel widening
Increased volume	*	*	*	*	*
Increased peak flow	*	*	*	*	*
Increased peak flow duration	*	*	*	*	*
Increased stream temperature		*			
Decreased base flow	*	*			
Changes in sediment loadings	*	*	*	*	*

Figure 1-1. Impacts from increases to impervious surfaces (USEPA 1997).

While impervious surfaces provide buildings and transportation networks, they have environmental costs beyond those from hydrologic and pollutant impacts. Other environmental impacts from impervious surfaces, especially impervious pavements, include (USEPA 2008):

- Urban Heat Island and increased air conditioning costs
- Air emissions from asphalt concrete and cement plants
- Air emissions from pavement construction and maintenance
- Decrease in green space
- Opportunity costs (i.e., forfeiting higher value uses)
- Degradation of community and neighborhood character

Best Management Practices (BMPs)

U.S. federal law (USEPA 2005) has mandated that states control non-point source water pollution through the National Pollution Discharge Elimination System (NPDES) program. The law requires, among many things, that states identify and require best management practices, or BMPs, to control non-point source pollution from new development. BMPs are implemented typically through regional and local governments charged with water quality management, planning, and regulation.

BMPs include many technologies and land management practices for reducing the quantity of pollutants in stormwater. They are used in combination at the site, development and watershed scales to attain the maximum benefits to the stormwater drainage system. BMPs are divided into structural and non-structural practices. Structural BMPs capture runoff and rely on gravitational settling and/or the infiltration through a porous medium for pollutant reduction.

They include detention dry ponds, wet (retention) ponds, infiltration trenches, sand filtration systems, and permeable pavements. These are often used to offset increases in pollutants caused by new development or decrease those from redevelopment.

Nonstructural BMPs involve a wider scope of practices. They can be public awareness programs about preventing non-point water pollution, street sweeping or the use of planning techniques such as riparian vegetative buffers. Many non-structural practices involve more efficient site planning. For example, these can include reducing the overall size of parking lots by reducing parking demand ratios, increasing shared parking, and use of mass transit credits. Many examples of nonstructural and structural practices can be found in *Better Site Design: A Handbook for Changing Development Rules in your Community* (CWP 1998).

In Canada, the Canadian Environmental Protection Act regulates many of the substances that have a deleterious effect on the environment including water pollutants in runoff. Recognizing the need for better environmental management, the Canadian federal government passed the Canada Water Act in 1970 and created the Department of the Environment in 1971, entrusting the Inland Waters Directorate with providing national leadership for freshwater management. Under the Constitution Act (1867), the provinces are "owners" of the water resources and have wide responsibilities in their day-to-day management.

The federal government has certain specific responsibilities relating to water, such as fisheries and navigation. While providing national leadership to ensure that Canada's freshwater management is in the national interest, Environment Canada also actively promotes a partnership approach among the various levels of government and private sector interests that contribute to, and benefit from, the wise management and sustainable use of this resource.

All of these interests were extensively consulted during the 1984-85 Inquiry on Federal Water Policy, which conducted Canada-wide hearings toward the development of a federal water policy. Guided by the findings of the Inquiry, the government released its Federal Water Policy in 1987 and it has given focus to all federal departments' water-related activities and provides a framework for future action as they evolve in light of new issues and concerns. Stormwater management is a growing concern at the federal, provincial and municipal levels. Infiltration practices and low impact development tools such as Permeable Interlocking Concrete Pavement (PICP) are increasing in use across Canada as a means to address those concerns.

PICP System Description

PICP is recognized by federal and state stormwater and transportation agencies as a BMP and low impact development (LID) tool to reduce runoff and water pollution. In addition, PICP offers unique design opportunities for creating green streets and parking lots as well as for reducing the urban heat island. Traditional stormwater management solutions focus on collecting, concentrating and centralizing the disposal of stormwater. As a key BMP and LID tool, PICP helps disconnect, decentralize and more widely distribute runoff through infiltration, detention, filtering and treatment.

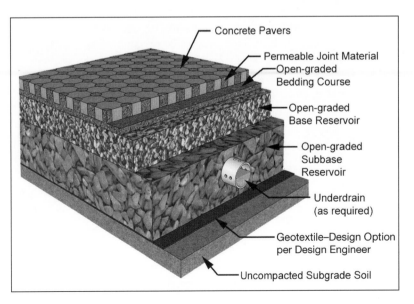

Figure 1-2 illustrates a typical PICP cross section. Solid concrete pavers with molded joints and/or openings create an open area across the pavement surface. Filled with permeable joint material, the openings allow water from storm events to freely enter the surface. Concrete pavers

Figure 1-2. PICP typical cross section. A description of each component is provided below.

Figure 1-3. Various types of paving units used in PICP

should conform to American Society for Testing and Materials, ASTM C 936 (ASTM 2009) in the U.S. or Canadian Standards Association, CSA A231.2 (CSA 2006) in Canada. Pavers are typically 3⅛ in. (80 mm) thick for vehicular areas and pedestrian areas may use 2⅜ in. (60 mm) thick units. Pavers are manufactured in a range of shapes and colors. Their surfaces can satisfy a minimum solar reflectance index or SRI of 29 per ASTM E 1980 (ASTM 2011). The units may include photocatalytic cement or pigment materials containing titanium oxide to reduce nitrous oxide air pollutants (Beeldens 2006). The traditional approach is that joints and/or openings comprise 5% to 15% of the paver surface (US EPA 2010) to provide sufficient drainage. However, research has shown that surface infiltration rates are a better way of defining permeable pavements. (This is covered in Section 2.) PICP surface infiltration relies on highly permeable, small-sized aggregates such as ASTM No. 8, 89 or 9 stone.[1] The permeable joints allow

---

[1]Numeric designations for jointing, bedding, open-graded base and subbase aggregate gradations used throughout this manual are found in ASTM D448 Standard Classification for Sizes of Aggregate for Road and Bridge Construction. The same gradations can be found in ASTM C33 Standard Specification for Concrete Aggregates or AASHTO M-43 Sizes of Aggregate for Road and Bridge Construction. Many of the referenced numeric designations for aggregates or similar ones are supplied by local quarries.

stormwater to enter a crushed stone, open-graded aggregate bedding course. Figure 1-3 shows several paver configurations.

Open-graded bedding course—This permeable layer is typically 2 in. (50 mm) thick and provides a level bed for the pavers. It consists of small-sized, open-graded aggregate, typically ASTM No. 8 stone or similar sized material.

Open-graded base reservoir—This is an aggregate layer 4 in. (100 mm) thick and made of crushed stones primarily 1 in. down to 1/2 in. (25 mm down to 13 mm). Besides storing water, this high infiltration rate layer provides a gradational transition between the bedding and subbase layers. The stone size is typically ASTM No. 57 or similar sized material.

Open-graded subbase reservoir—The stone sizes are larger than the base, primarily 3 in. down to 2 in. (75 mm down to 50 mm), typically ASTM No. 2, 3 or 4 stone. Like the base layer, water is stored in the spaces among the stones. The subbase layer thickness depends on water storage requirements and traffic loads (covered in Section 3). A subbase layer may not be required in pedestrian or residential driveway applications. In such instances, the base layer thickness is increased to provide water storage and support.

Underdrain (as required)—In sites where PICP is installed over low-infiltration soils underdrains facilitate water removal from the base and subbase. The underdrains are perforated pipes that "daylight" to a swale or stream, or connect to an outlet structure. Pipe elevation, spacing, diameter and slope will impact outflow volumes and rates from connected PICP. Another design option to which underdrains connect are plastic or concrete vaults or plastic crates. These can store significant amounts of runoff.

Geotextile (design option per engineer)—This can separate the subbase from the subgrade and prevent migration of soil into the aggregate subbase or base. A detailed discussion on this option is presented in Section 3.

Subgrade—The layer of soil immediately beneath the aggregate base or subbase. The infiltration rate of the saturated subgrade determines how much water can exfiltrate from the aggregate into the underlying soils. The subgrade soil is generally not compacted as this can substantially reduce soil infiltration. However, some poorly draining clay soils are often compacted to help ensure structural stability especially when saturated. Since compaction reduces infiltration, managing the excess water must be considered in the hydrologic design via the base/subbase thickness and use of perforated pipe underdrains. This is covered in Sections 2 and 3.

Concrete Grid Pavements—PICP should not be confused with concrete grid pavements, concrete units with cells that typically contain topsoil and grass. See Figure 1-4. These paving units can infiltrate water, but at substantially lower rates than PICP usually similar to that of a grassed surface. Unlike PICP, concrete grid pavements are typically designed with a dense-graded, crushed stone base rather than an open-graded base for water storage. Moreover, grids are for light-duty use, i.e., intermittently trafficked areas such as overflow parking areas and emergency fire lanes for fire trucks. Grid pavements are not intended for regularly used parking lots or roads whereas PICP is well-suited for these applications. Grids with grass offer substantial cooling compared to hard surfaces. Grid pavement design and construction requirements differ substantially from PICP. See *ICPI Tech Spec 8–Concrete Grid Pavements* which provides detailed information (ICPI 2006).

Figure 1-4. Concrete grid pavements are a permeable pavement but are used in intermittently trafficked areas.

Figure 1-5. Ferdinand Street in Chicago is paved with PICP as part of a city redevelopment project.

Figure 1-6. Approximately 1.5 miles (2.4 km) of PICP serves Main Street in Warrenville, Illinois.

Figure 1-7. Elmhurst College, Elmhurst, Illinois uses PICP for runoff control and water harvesting.

Figure 1-8. The Snoqualmie, Washington fire station uses PICP in the entrance driveway.

PICP Applications

PICP is used as a standard pavement (replacing impervious pavements) by municipalities for stormwater management programs and in private developments. The runoff volume, rate and pollutant reductions allow municipalities to meet federal, provincial, state and local regulatory water quality criteria. Municipal initiatives such as the Chicago Department of Transportation Green Alley program and Portland, Oregon, used PICP to reduce combined sewer overflows (CSO) and minimize localized flooding by infiltrating and treating stormwater on site. Green alley pilot projects by the City of Richmond, Virginia, Los Angeles, California, Philadelphia, Pennsylvania and Washington, DC store and slowly release water to reduce peak flows, as well as filter pollutants, as a CSO reduction tool. The City of Chicago and Warrenville, Illinois use PICP for low-volume streets in residential and redeveloped industrial areas. Figures 1-5 and 1-6 illustrate these projects.

Private commercial and residential development projects use PICP to meet post-construction stormwater quantity and quality regulations and low impact development ordinances. Universities, colleges (Figure 1-7), public schools, fire stations (Figure 1-8), libraries, museums, and stadiums use PICP to reduce runoff and achieve sustainable site design objectives.

Municipalities are using PICP to replace traditional impervious pavement for pedestrian and vehicular applications except for high-volume/high-speed roadways. PICP has performed successfully in pedestrian walkways, sidewalks, driveways, parking lots, and low-volume roadways subject to truck traffic. The environmental benefits from PICP

Figure 1-9. Park 542, also known as Mary Bartelme Park, located in Chicago's West Loop includes PICP with a white titanium oxide cement to help reduce air pollutants.

Figure 1-10. Autumn Trails in Moline, Illinois used 39,000 sf (3,900 m²) of PICP without storm sewers making it cost-competitive with conventional paving with drainage.

allow it to be incorporated into municipal green infrastructure and low impact development (LID) programs. PICP is a key element in the LID "treatment train" approach that seeks to maximize on-site infiltration. In addition to providing stormwater volume and quality management, light colored pavers are cooler than conventional asphalt. This helps reduce urban summer temperatures and improve air quality by using photocatalytic materials made with titanium dioxide. An example is shown in Figure 1-9. The textured surface of PICP also provides traffic calming and provides a context sensitive, visually unifying appearance.

Economics—PICP can be cost-effective in new development and redevelopment. Cost savings in new projects arise from on-site infiltration that reduces or eliminates, storm sewers, detention/retention ponds, making more land available for buildings. An example of cost savings in residential roads is Autumn Trails community in Moline, Illinois. About 39,000 sf (3,900 m²) in PICP eliminated the need for storm sewer inlets and pipes. Figure 1-10 illustrates the project.

According to developer estimates, PICP without storm sewer drainage was cost-competitive with conventional pavements using standard drainage systems (2006 prices). Cost comparisons include identical curbing for all pavements and appropriate base materials and thicknesses.

Pavement System	PICP no sewers	Concrete w/ sewers	Asphalt w/ sewers
Cost/sf (m²)	$10.95 ($117.82)	$15.00 ($161.40)	$11.50 ($123.74)

Another source of savings emerges from local regulations that limit the total amount of impervious cover. Savings comes from permeable pavement counted as pervious land cover which can enable a larger building footprint on the site and greater sales or rental income. In the presence or absence of local impervious cover (i.e., roofs and paving) limitations, the higher cost of PICP compared to conventional paving may be recovered from increased income from more buildings or from more rentable space in buildings. Sites should be evaluated for these economic trade-offs of pavement system choices, stormwater management options, and building space.

Figure 1-11. The parking lot at this retail center in Burnaby, BC provides the retention and filtering of water from the adjacent roofs as well as from the parking lot.

Within existing urban redevelopment projects, PICP is particularly cost-effective when parking areas need expansion but there is no space for detention ponds or existing ones cannot be expanded. In some projects, low-slope building roofs (or vegetated roofs) can serve as detention and transfer the water into the permeable pavement. This is the case in a shopping center in Burnaby, British Columbia as shown in Figure 1-11. The water from the roofs is directed into the base under the 350,000 sf (35,000 m2) PICP surface which covers the entire parking lot. There are no storm sewer inlets in the parking lot since the entire surface functions as one.

Many urban areas suffer from storm sewers operating at capacity and flooding in high rainfall events. An increasing number of local governments are requiring PICP for new or rebuilt residential and commercial pavements. A few local governments provide financial incentives to residential and commercial property owners to convert impervious pavement to permeable pavement. Examples include Montgomery County, MD and Palo Alto, CA. Both municipalities offer rebates to land owners for installing a range of methods to reduce stormwater including PICP. In both jurisdictions, replacing existing storm sewers with larger ones to reduce flooding was not economical. Therefore, providing financial incentives to land owners that help transform the earth's surface from impervious to PICP is offered as a less expensive solution for the municipality.

PICP Benefits

Construction

- Immediately ready for traffic upon completion, no additional time needed for curing
- Can be installed in cold weather if subgrade and aggregates remain unfrozen
- Capable of wet weather (light rain) installation
- No time-sensitive materials that require site forming and management for curing
- Contractor training and credentials available through ICPI

Reduced Runoff

- Up to 100% surface runoff reduction (subject to design requirements)
- Up to 100% infiltration depending on the design and soil subgrade infiltration rate
- Capable of installation over or next to plastic underground storage vaults or crates
- Can be designed with water harvesting systems for site irrigation and gray water uses

Improved Water Quality

- Reduces nutrients, metals and oils
- Does not raise runoff temperature which can damage aquatic life
- Can be used as to achieve water quality capture volume
- Can be used to achieve total maximum daily load (TMDL) limits for a range of pollutants

Site Utilization

- Reduces or eliminates unsightly detention/retention ponds
- Increased site and building utilization
- Conservation of space on the site and reduction of impervious cover
- Preserves woods and open space that would have been destroyed for detention ponds
- Promotes tree survival by providing air and water to roots (roots do not heave pavement)

Drainage System

- Reduced downstream flows and stream bank erosion due to decreased peak flows and volumes
- Increased recharge of groundwater
- Decreases risk of salt water incursion and drinking water well pollution in coastal areas
- Reduced peak discharges and stress on storm sewers
- Reduces combined sanitary/storm sewer overflows

Reduced Operating Costs

- Reduced overall project costs due to reducing or eliminating storm sewers and drainage appurtenances
- Lower life-cycle costs than conventional pavements
- Capable of integration with horizontal ground source heat pumps to reduce building heating and cooling energy costs
- Enables landowner credits on stormwater utility fees
- Does not require sealing which lowers maintenance costs

Paver surface/units

- 50-year design life based on proven field performance
- ADA compliant
- Colored units can mark parking stalls and driving lanes; light colors can reduce night time lighting needs
- Eliminates puddles on parking lots, walkways, entrances, etc.
- Capable of plowing with municipal snow removal equipment
- Durable, high-strength, low-absorption concrete units resist freeze-thaw, heaving and degradation from deicing materials
- Reduced ice and deicing material use/costs due to rapid ice melt and surface infiltration
- Reduced liability from slipping on ice due to rapid ice melt and surface infiltration
- Provides traffic calming
- Paver surface can be coated with photocatalytic materials to reduce air pollution
- High solar reflectance index (SRI) surface helps reduce micro-climatic temperatures and contributes to urban heat island reduction
- Units manufactured with recycled materials and cement substitutes to reduce greenhouse gas emissions

Ease of Maintenance & Repairs

- Paving units and base materials can be removed and reinstated
- Utility cuts into the pavement do not damage the surface and decrease pavement life
- Capable of winter repairs
- No unsightly patches from utility cuts
- Surface cleaning with standard vacuum equipment
- Clogged surfaces may be restored with vacuum equipment to reinstate infiltration rates

LEED® version 3 Credits (USGBC 2009)

Within the North American design and construction community, a means for addressing sustainability or green building is through LEED® or Leadership in Energy and Environmental Design. Developed by the U.S. Green Building Council (USGBC) in 1998, LEED® provides voluntary guidelines for reducing energy and wasted resources from building and sites. Projects earn points toward varying certification levels. PICP earns points under several LEED® credit categories using the U.S. and Canadian Green Building Councils (USGBC and CaGBC) guidelines. These are enumerated below.

Sustainable Sites

		Points
Credit 6.1	Stormwater Design: Quantity Control	1
Credit 6.2	Stormwater Design: Quality Control	1
Credit 7.1	Heat Island Effect: Non-Roof	1
Credit 7.2	Heat Island Effect: Roof	1

Water Efficiency

		Points
Credit 1	Water Efficient Landscaping: Reduce by 50% (water harvesting)	2
	No Potable Water Use or Irrigation (water harvesting)	4

Energy & Atmosphere

		Points
Credit 2	On-site Renewable Energy (PICP w/ground source heat pump)	1-7

Materials and Resources (applies to entire project)

		Points
Credit 2	Construction Waste Management - Recycled or Salvaged: 50%	1
	Construction Waste Management - Recycled or Salvaged: 75%	2
Credit 3	Materials Reuse: 5%	1
	Materials Reuse: 10%	2
Credit 4	Recycled content: 10%	1
	Recycled content: 20%	2
Credit 5	Regional materials: 10%	1
	Regional materials: 20%	2

Innovation and Design

		Points
Credit 1	Path 1 - Innovation in Design (e.g. TiO_2 materials for air pollution reduction)	1-5
	Path 2 – Exemplary Performance	1-3

Life Cycle Assessment

An emerging consideration in sustainable rating systems such as LEED® is life cycle assessment or LCA for environmental impact and environmental performance analyses. LCA is described in detail in the ISO 14000 series of standards. LCA includes goal and scope definition, inventory analysis, impact assessment, and interpretation of social, environment and economic impacts of a project. These impacts are weighted and justified as part of the analysis. Potential impacts analyzed include:

- Global warming (from greenhouse gases)
- Acidification (typically from acid rain)
- Eutrophication (accelerated aging of water bodies through excess nutrient intake)
- Fossil fuel depletion
- Indoor air quality
- Habitat alternation
- Water intake
- Air pollutants and smog
- Ecological toxicity
- Ozone depletion
- Human health

Local, state and federal transportation agencies, as well as private sector project owners, are adopting LCA as a means to reduce waste, pollutants, and environmental, social and economic costs to the project and the wider society. PICP offers a range of environmental, economic and social benefits that can reduce the above impacts during manufacture, construction and especially over its life cycle.

Sustainable Rating Systems for Roadways

An emerging area that parallels LEED® and LCA is sustainable rating systems for design, construction and use of roadways. These rating systems provide transportation agencies with checklists and analytical tools similar to LEED® and LCA but with greater emphasis on site, user, wider community and road system impacts. Roadway sustainability rating systems typically consider and rate the aspects listed below. These are used to compare and influence investment decisions in pavement systems, roadway design and routes:

- Environmental review process including LCA
- Life cycle energy use inventory (as input to LCA) for materials and construction
- Life cycle cost analysis or LCCA (construction and maintenance costs, plus user delay costs due to maintenance)
- Construction quality control plans
- Noise mitigation
- Waste management
- Stormwater runoff management and low-impact development principles
- Pavement management systems and maintenance plans
- Educational outreach to the stakeholder community(ies)

PICP again positively addresses several of these aspects.

Section 2. Design Contexts, Overview and Guidelines

Municipal Stormwater Management Objectives

Municipal drainage and low-impact development ordinances vary widely. Factors influencing them include geomorphology, water supply needs, water laws, rainfall patterns, development and redevelopment pressures, carrying capacity of the natural drainage or man-made storm sewer system, as well as the receiving water capacity to process pollutants and excessive water volumes. Many regional authorities, drainage districts, counties, cities and towns aim at preserving natural drainage and treatment systems or limit flows to drainage systems especially if they are working at capacity. Integration of low-impact development principles into many state/provincial and municipal regulations has increased focus on reducing runoff volumes which results in pollutant reductions.

A well-structured municipal stormwater management strategy will use a range of post-construction BMPs that address runoff reduction and water quality improvement. Regulatory approaches implement BMPs that incorporate some or all of the following water quality and water quantity goals.

1. Reduce generation of additional stormwater and pollutants by restricting the growth of impervious surfaces. This approach can embrace one or more goals that include:

   • Recharge groundwater for maintaining stream base flows
   • Recharge aquifers used for drinking water
   • Relieve combined sewer overflows in older urban areas
   • Protect nearby high-value (drinking water supply, recreation or fishing) body of water from pollution
   • Reduce runoff volumes to control local flooding from the natural drainage system or from storm sewers operating at capacity.

2. Treat (i.e., detain and infiltrate) runoff from commonly recurring storms to remove a given percentage of pollutants from the average annual post-development load. This approach is sometimes called "water quality volume capture." Target pollutant reductions typically include total suspended solids (TSS), total phosphorous (TP) and/or total nitrogen (TN) as these are primary indicators of water quality. Pollutant levels are measured in sewers, streams and other natural water bodies on reduction of mass or of event mean concentrations.

3. Reduce specific pollutants to lower levels for processing by a receiving body of water. Pollutant emissions are sometimes reduced to levels a receiving body of water (e.g. stream, lake, estuary, bay, etc.) can process without incurring further damage to the aquatic ecosystem and especially to its economic value. This approach to limiting pollutants from a watershed is often called total maximum daily load or TMDL restrictions and there is an increasing number of U.S. watersheds subject such restrictions. This approach can rely on documented relationships between land uses and runoff subject to such pollutant loads.

   Other regulatory approaches manage stormwater in a hierarchy of rainfall events according to recurrence level with strategies to manage increasing depths, volumes, flows and resulting environmental

impacts. The hierarchy manages runoff volumes and flow criteria based on their potential for pollution and flooding. The approach is typically structured in ascending order of storm depths as follows:

(a) Capture and treat a specific water quality volume defined as the initial depth of rainfall on a site (usually ranging from 0.75 in to 1.5 in. or 19 to 40 mm). The depth is expressed as a percentage of all storms that can range between 75% and 95%. This approach often controls runoff from commonly recurring storms (up to one year recurrence) since they generally contain the highest concentration of pollutants, similar to number 2 above.

(b) Enhance stream channel protection through extended detention and infiltration of runoff volumes from a given storm event, e.g., a 1 or 2 year 24-hour storm. The difference in volumes between pre- and post development is often detained, infiltrated and/or slowly released. Sometimes there is agency-developer debate on what type of land cover and resulting runoff constitutes a "pre-development" condition. Streambank protection is regulated through techniques that dissipate water energy and velocity in streams and through preservation of vegetative buffers along streams.

(c) Reduce overbank flooding in streams through reducing the post-development peak discharge rate to the pre-development rate for larger storms such as a 25-year, 24-hour event.

(d) Reduce the risk of extreme flooding by controlling and/or safely conveying the 100-year, 24-hour return frequency storm event. This goal is also supported by preserving existing and future floodplain areas from development or restricting it in them as much as possible.

Figure 2-1 schematically illustrates how PICP can help address most of the above regulatory goals. PICP is most effective in managing runoff from commonly recurring storms and can be designed to help manage less infrequent, higher depth storms. In most parts of North America, commonly recurring storms comprise 75% to 95% of all rain events. If designed to store less frequent, bigger storms runoff volumes and/or discharge rates can be decreased with PICP to help reduce erosion of drainage channels. While having some limited benefits, increased storage capacity of rainfall volume in the base can contribute some local flood control.

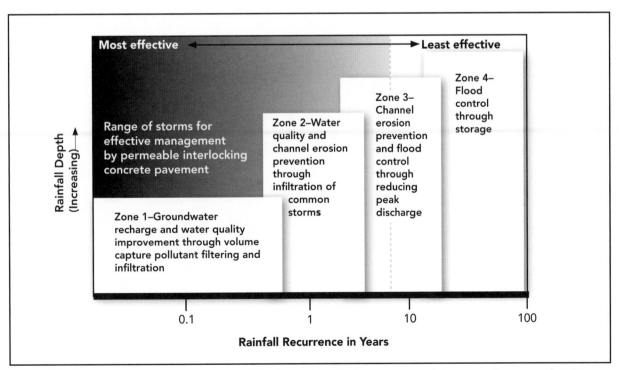

Figure 2-1. Various stormwater management objectives related to the spectrum of storms can be met with PICP (after Claytor 1996).

Impervious Cover Restrictions, Stormwater Utilities and PICP

An increasing number of municipalities regulate the amount of impervious cover on a range of land uses. Restrictions can be based on not exceeding the maximum capacity of storm sewers and streams to handle runoff from existing impervious surfaces without flooding and property damage. In other cases, severe restrictions (e.g., <15% impervious cover) are enacted to preserve fish habitats or nearby natural resources (e.g., natural area next to a stream, estuary or bay) or to stop local flooding from worsening.

Since impervious surfaces are the primary cause of drainage system damage, impervious cover restrictions are the most effective means to reduce runoff volumes and pollutants. In such cases, provincial/state and municipal regulations often credit PICP as a permeable or pervious surface when some or all of the water for given design storms is infiltrated into soil subgrade. Reduction or elimination of impervious pavement using PICP has a two-fold benefit depending on local development objectives. PICP can facilitate conservation of existing natural areas or enable larger building/roof area. Roofs can be designed to sustain vegetation on it (green roof), capture water for irrigating site vegetation, or simply detain and slowly release water. Additional houses or commercial buildings can readily offset the additional expense for PICP.

Another approach that establishes a legal, technical and municipal administrative framework for managing municipal drainage infrastructure is the stormwater utility. Over 1,300 municipalities have created stormwater utilities similar to existing water and sewer utilities. The legal rationale for a stormwater utility is rain that falls on private property belongs to the property owner. Therefore, removal of runoff from private property through a publicly-owned municipal drainage system should be paid as a user fee by the property owner to the local municipal utility (similar to sanitary waste or trash removal). The fee charged by the municipality for this service depends on how much runoff is discharged from each property. The fee is often based on the percent of impervious cover, land use (i.e., zoning), or local government need to capitalize and maintain a storm drainage system. A residential property owner pays a lower fee while a shopping center owner pays a higher one due to generating more runoff from a higher area of roofs and parking lots.

In most cases, the fees go specifically to managing stormwater. Therefore, the charge to property owners is not considered a tax which pays for a wider range of municipal services. Typically, stormwater utility fees are used by the municipality for maintaining and expanding the municipal drainage system. In some instances, fees are also used to restore damaged streams and riparian habitats, thereby reinstating lost or damaged riparian property and natural or recreational amenities.

Some stormwater utility fee structures offer a discount or credit to land owners that reduce runoff entering the municipal drainage system. An owner's fee may be reduced if there is reduction of impermeable surfaces using permeable pavement or if the water is stored on the owner's site. Since PICP offers storage and infiltration, a strong rationale exists for reduction of stormwater utility fees. Reese (Reese 2007) offers additional rationale for credits to stormwater utility fees.

Some regulatory agencies achieve volume and pollutant reductions through comprehensive stormwater management, operation and maintenance plan funded and administered through stormwater utilities. Larger municipalities or those with stormwater utilities can operate computational models to forecast development impacts on the publicly owned drainage system. While the Rational Method persists in many places due to its simplicity, some governments and design consultants use more sophisticated stormwater modeling and field calibration of watersheds and watercourses in their jurisdictions. Models can range from NRCS (USDA 2003) or more sophisticated continuous simulation models such as HEC or EPA SWMM, WINSLAM, a water balance/budget or agency-specific models. These results inform drainage guidelines for specific site development proposals. Sophisticated modeling can also simulate downstream impacts (i.e., stream bank erosion and flooding) from a specific development proposal. Before modeling hydrologic aspects, the following covers fundamental concepts in PICP design.

PICP System Basics

Site Selection Criteria—PICP is recommended in areas with the following site characteristics:

Figure 2-2. A large PICP parking lot manages an overall site slope of 12% using terraced areas.

- Residential patios, walks and driveways.
- Walks, parking lots, main and service driveways around commercial, institutional, recreational and cultural buildings.
- Low speed (<40 mph or 65 kph) residential roads.
- Non-commercial boat landings and marinas.
- Industrial sites that do not receive hazardous materials, i.e., where there is no risk to groundwater or soils from spills.
- Storage areas for shipping containers with non-hazardous contents.
- Runoff from contributing at-grade impervious areas does not exceed five times the area of the PICP receiving the runoff.
- The estimated depth from the bottom of the pavement base to the seasonal high level of the water table is greater than 2 feet (0.6 m). Greater depths may be required to obtain additional filtering of pollutants through the soil.
- PICP is downslope from building foundations and the foundations have piped drainage at the footers. Waterproofing such as an impermeable liner is recommended on basement walls against PICP.
- The slope of the permeable pavement surface is at least 1% and no greater than 12%. Figure 2-2 illustrates a large unique PICP parking lot near Atlanta, Georgia with a slope of 12% across the site. PICP surface slopes are typically 5% or less. There should be a minimum 1% surface slope to enable removal of water in the extreme case of the entire system filling with water such that it emerges from the surface.
- Land surrounding and draining into the PICP does not exceed 20% slope.
- At least 100 ft (30 m) should be maintained between PICP and municipal water supply wells. (Local jurisdictions may provide additional guidance or regulations.)
- Sites where the owner can meet maintenance requirements (see maintenance section).
- Sites where runoff draining onto PICP surface is not from soil erosion, exposed topsoil or mulch.
- Sites where there will not be an increase in impervious cover draining into the PICP (unless the pavement is designed to infiltrate and store runoff from future increases in impervious cover due to future development).
- Sites where space constraints, high land prices, tree/green space conservation, land used by detention facilities, and/or runoff from additional development make PICP a cost-effective solution.
- Sites outside permafrost regions

PICP can be designed with full, partial or no exfiltration of the open-graded stone base into the soil subgrade. Details on each follow.

Full and Partial Exfiltration—Full exfiltration directs water through the base/subbase and exfiltrates it to the soil subgrade. This is the most common application over high infiltration soils such as gravels and sands. Overflows are managed via perimeter drains to swales, bio-retention areas or storm sewer inlets. Figure 2-3 illustrates schematic cross section of a full exfiltration PICP. Overflow drainage can exit from the surface but is better managed via large drainpipes from within the base. Subsurface drainage can help prevent mobilization of sediment trapped in the PICP openings. Figure 2-4 illustrates an example of handling PICP overflows via curb inlets to bioswales.

PICP is not recommended on any site classified as a stormwater hotspot, i.e., if there is any risk that stormwater can infiltrate and contaminate groundwater. These land uses and activities may include the following:

- Vehicle salvage yards, recycling facilities, fueling stations, service and maintenance facilities, equipment and cleaning facilities
- Fleet storage areas (bus, truck, etc.)
- Commercial marina service and maintenance areas
- Outdoor liquid container storage areas
- Outdoor unloading facilities in industrial areas
- Public works materials/equipment storage areas
- Industrial facilities that generate or store hazardous materials
- Storage areas for commercial shipping containers with contents that could damage ground-water and soil
- Land uses that drain pesticides and/or fertilizers into permeable pavements (e.g., agricultural land, etc.)
- Other land uses and activities as designated by an appropriate review authority

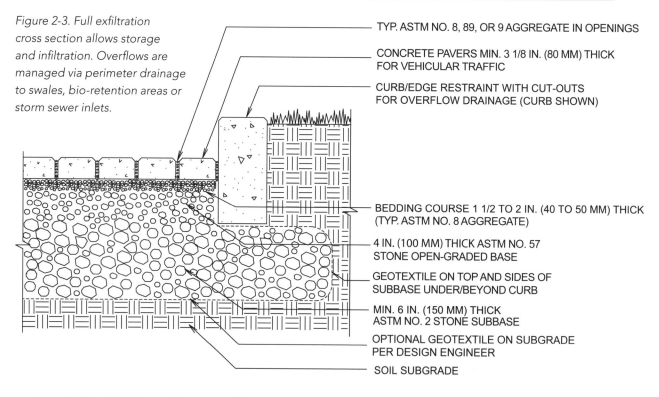

Figure 2-3. Full exfiltration cross section allows storage and infiltration. Overflows are managed via perimeter drainage to swales, bio-retention areas or storm sewer inlets.

TYP. ASTM NO. 8, 89, OR 9 AGGREGATE IN OPENINGS

CONCRETE PAVERS MIN. 3 1/8 IN. (80 MM) THICK FOR VEHICULAR TRAFFIC

CURB/EDGE RESTRAINT WITH CUT-OUTS FOR OVERFLOW DRAINAGE (CURB SHOWN)

BEDDING COURSE 1 1/2 TO 2 IN. (40 TO 50 MM) THICK (TYP. ASTM NO. 8 AGGREGATE)

4 IN. (100 MM) THICK ASTM NO. 57 STONE OPEN-GRADED BASE

GEOTEXTILE ON TOP AND SIDES OF SUBBASE UNDER/BEYOND CURB

MIN. 6 IN. (150 MM) THICK ASTM NO. 2 STONE SUBBASE

OPTIONAL GEOTEXTILE ON SUBGRADE PER DESIGN ENGINEER

SOIL SUBGRADE

Figure 2-4. Elmhurst College, Elmhurst, Illinois parking lots uses full exfiltration through the soil subgrade with overflows directed through curb inlets into bio-retention areas and overflow drains to manage extreme rain events.

Partial exfiltration relies on drainage of the base/subbase into the subgrade soil and drainage pipes to direct excess water to a sewer or a stream. This controls the amount of time the subgrade is saturated. This design is common to lower infiltration rate soils such as silts and clays. Perforated drain pipes are typically raised some inches (cm) above the soil subgrade to allow some water capture and infiltration into the soil subgrade below them. When the water level rises to the pipes it drains away through them. An alternative approach places perforated pipes at the bottom of the subbase drained via riser pipes or sumps. The vertical riser pipes turn horizontal without perforations to drain accumulated water. See Figure 4-16. When perforated drain pipes are raised, water is typically detained for 24 to 48 hours which can enable nutrient reduction through de-nitrification similar to that in detention ponds. Soils with infiltration rates as low as 0.01 in./hr (7×10^{-6} cm/sec) can infiltrate about 0.5 in. (13 mm) over 48 hours. Therefore, this

Figure 2-5. Partial exfiltration through the soil subgrade. Perforated pipes can be raised above the soil subgrade to drain water from higher depth rainstorms. Smaller storms which often contain higher pollutant concentrations can be captured below the perforated pipes, stored and infiltrated.

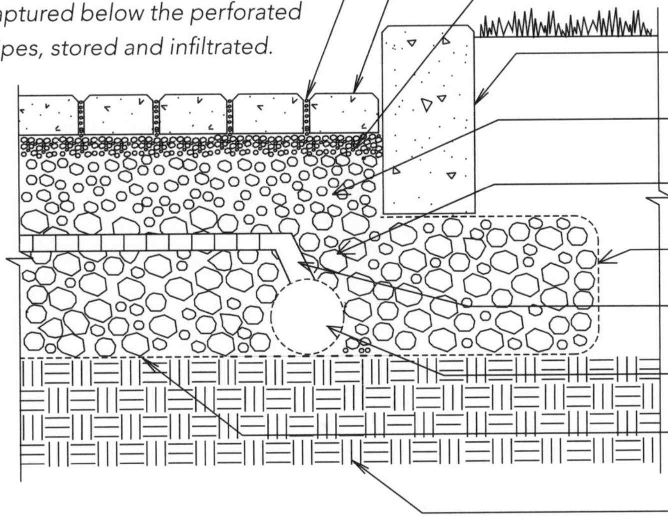

TYP. ASTM NO. 8, 89, OR 9 AGGREGATE IN OPENINGS

CONCRETE PAVERS MIN. 3 1/8 IN. (80 MM) THICK FOR VEHICULAR TRAFFIC

BEDDING COURSE 1 1/2 IN. TO 2 IN. (40 TO 50 MM) THICK (TYP. ASTM NO. 8 AGGREGATE)

CURB/EDGE RESTRAINT WITH CUT-OUTS FOR OVERFLOW DRAINAGE (CURB SHOWN)

4 IN. (100 MM) THICK ASTM NO. 57 STONE OPEN-GRADED BASE

MIN. 6 IN. (150 MM) THICK ASTM NO. 2 STONE SUBBASE

GEOTEXTILE ON TOP AND SIDES OF SUBBASE UNDER/BEYOND CURB

PERFORATED PIPES SPACED AND SLOPED TO DRAIN EXCESS WATER

NON-PERFORATED OUTFALL PIPE(S) SLOPED TO STORM SEWER OR STREAM

GEOTEXTILE ON SUBGRADE PER DESIGN ENGINEER

SOIL SUBGRADE SURFACE SLOPED TO DRAIN

Figure 2-6. Partial exfiltration designs typically use perforated pipes raised above the soil subgrade. This enables capture and infiltration of some runoff.

design approach can be used in some clay soils. Figure 2-5 illustrates a schematic cross-section of partial exfiltration design and Figure 2-6 shows a perforated pipe raised over the soil subgrade.

Partial exfiltration designs have also been successfully used in coastal areas and islands where the depth to the water table is close to the surface with little slope to drain bases. PICP structures have been designed with sufficiently thick bases to support vehicular traffic while water occupies the lower portion of the aggregate subbase over a sandy subgrade. The sandy soil remains stable while saturated and the base/subbase mitigates stresses from loads to the soil. Drain pipes provided at higher elevations within the base remove excess water when the water table rises from rainfall and tidal surges. Drain

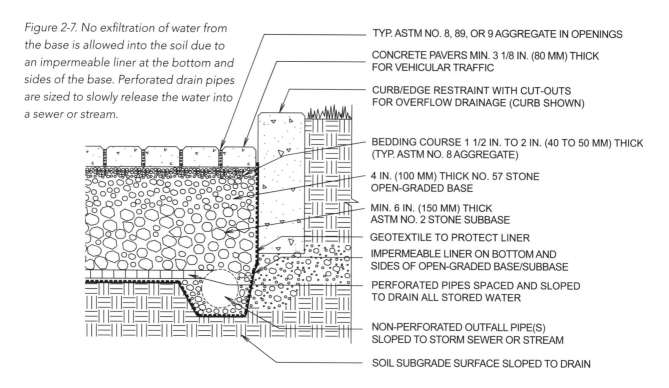

Figure 2-7. No exfiltration of water from the base is allowed into the soil due to an impermeable liner at the bottom and sides of the base. Perforated drain pipes are sized to slowly release the water into a sewer or stream.

TYP. ASTM NO. 8, 89, OR 9 AGGREGATE IN OPENINGS

CONCRETE PAVERS MIN. 3 1/8 IN. (80 MM) THICK FOR VEHICULAR TRAFFIC

CURB/EDGE RESTRAINT WITH CUT-OUTS FOR OVERFLOW DRAINAGE (CURB SHOWN)

BEDDING COURSE 1 1/2 IN. TO 2 IN. (40 TO 50 MM) THICK (TYP. ASTM NO. 8 AGGREGATE)

4 IN. (100 MM) THICK NO. 57 STONE OPEN-GRADED BASE

MIN. 6 IN. (150 MM) THICK ASTM NO. 2 STONE SUBBASE

GEOTEXTILE TO PROTECT LINER

IMPERMEABLE LINER ON BOTTOM AND SIDES OF OPEN-GRADED BASE/SUBBASE

PERFORATED PIPES SPACED AND SLOPED TO DRAIN ALL STORED WATER

NON-PERFORATED OUTFALL PIPE(S) SLOPED TO STORM SEWER OR STREAM

SOIL SUBGRADE SURFACE SLOPED TO DRAIN

pipes are usually connected to a storm sewer. This design approach can address salt water incursion in coastal areas by maintaining needed fresh water in groundwater aquifers which blocks incursion of less dense salt water.

No Exfiltration

No exfiltration is required when the soil has very low permeability and low strength, or there are other site limitations. The assembly is a detention pond with an outlet. An impermeable liner may be used if the pollutant loads are expected to exceed the capacity of the base/subbase and soil subgrade to treat them. The liner can be high density polyethylene (HDPE), ethylene propylene diene monomer (EPDM) or polyvinyl chloride (PVC). Manufacturers of these materials should be consulted for appropriate applications, thicknesses, specifications and field construction guidance including seam welding, and how to render a tight fit against penetrating drain pipes. Liners typically require geotextile over them for additional protection during aggregate filling and compaction. No exfiltration is also used for creating a reservoir for water harvesting or horizontal ground source heat pumps that augment nearby building heating and cooling needs.

A minimum 1 ft (0.3 m) clearance is recommended between the bottom of the impermeable liner and the seasonal high water table. Figure 2-7 illustrates a cross-section design for no exfiltration into the soil subgrade. In some cases, the soil may be stabilized to render improved support for vehicular loads rather than using an impermeable liner. This practice reduces soil infiltration to practically zero and provides additional stability in saturated conditions. Figure 2-8 shows an impermeable liner with geotextile around a PICP subbase.

No exfiltration designs with impermeable liners are recommended in the following sites:

Figure 2-8. The bottom and sides of this PICP subbase is enclosed with an EPDM impermeable liner and geotextile to capture, filter and eventually drain runoff through the subbase via an underdrain.

- Over aquifers with insufficient soil depth to filter the pollutants before entering the ground water. These can include karst, fissured or cleft aquifers.
- Over fill soils whose behavior when exposed to infiltrating water may cause unacceptable settling and movement. These might include expansive soils such as loess, poorly compacted soils, gypsiferous soils, etc.

In rare cases, soil directly below the subbase may be low-infiltration clay while soils further down may offer increased infiltration. It may be cost-effective to drain the water via a vertical French drain or pipes through the impermeable layer of soil into the lower soil layer with greater permeability.

In the US, the Safe Drinking Water Act regulates the infiltration of stormwater in certain situations pursuant to the Underground Injection Control (UIC) Program administered by the US EPA or a delegated state groundwater protection agency. This program divides wells into five classes depending on their design and use. According to EPA, "Class V wells are shallow disposal systems that depend on gravity to drain fluids directly in the ground...Most of these Class V wells are unsophisticated shallow disposal systems that include storm water drainage wells, cesspools, and septic system leach fields. However, the Class V well category also includes more complex wells that are typically deeper and often used at commercial or industrial facilities." The EPA (EPA 2008) determined that permeable pavement installations are not classified as Class V injection wells, since they are always wider than they are deep.

Handling Sloped Sites

Soil subgrades can be bermed and piped to control downslope flows and encourage infiltration. Figures 2-9 and 2-10 illustrates two options for sloped PICP applications; stepped and sloped installations. These approaches maximize water storage and help reduce subbase thickness not used for water storage.

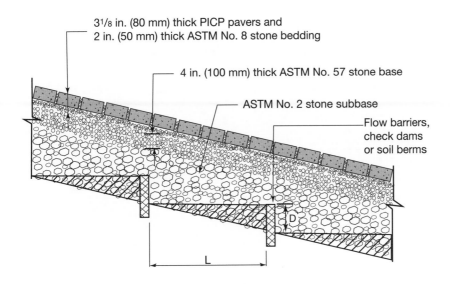

3 1/8 in. (80 mm) thick PICP pavers and 2 in. (50 mm) thick ASTM No. 8 stone bedding

4 in. (100 mm) thick ASTM No. 57 stone base

ASTM No. 2 stone subbase

Flow barriers, check dams or soil berms

Figure 2-9. PICP stepped installation. Designs with subgrade slopes over 3% should consider flow barriers, check dams or soil berms.

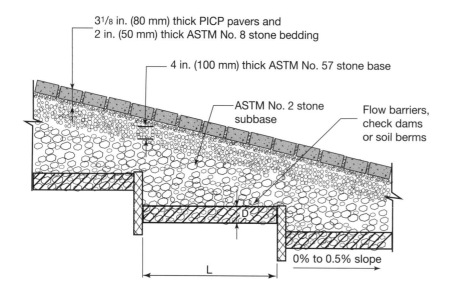

3¹⁄₈ in. (80 mm) thick PICP pavers and
2 in. (50 mm) thick ASTM No. 8 stone bedding

4 in. (100 mm) thick ASTM No. 57 stone base

ASTM No. 2 stone subbase

Flow barriers, check dams or soil berms

L

D

0% to 0.5% slope

Figure 2-10. PICP sloped installation. The design assumes slope to the soil subgrade with barriers to slow down flow. Barriers can be soil berms (non-excavated soil subgrade), concrete curbs, geotextile over impervious geomembrane, aggregate wrapped in geotextile, etc. Slowing the flow through the barriers via drain pipes is recommended.

Formulas are provided to estimate water storage between barriers or soil berms:

$$V = P \times \frac{D\,A}{2} \quad \text{(Figure 2-9)}$$

Where:
V = Volume available in the reservoir (cf)
P = Porosity of the aggregate base/subbase (e.g., 0.4)
D = Maximum depth of the reservoir at the barrier (ft)
A = Horizontal surface area of the PICP between barriers (sf) or L x pavement width

$$V = P\,D\,A \quad \text{(Figure 2-10)}$$

Where:
V= Volume available in the reservoir (cf)
P = Porosity of the aggregate base/subbase (e.g., 0.4)
D = Depth of reservoir portion of the base between barriers (ft)
A = Horizontal surface area of the PICP between barriers (sf) or L x pavement width

Design Considerations for Disabled Persons

PICP complies with the Americans with Disabilities Act (ADA) design guidelines provided that surfaces within accessible paths of travel routes on sites meet the following criteria (DOJ 2010):

- Firm, stable and slip resistant.
- An unacceptable opening is one that can receive insertion of a ½ in. (13 mm) steel sphere. PICP openings filled with small aggregate (typically to the bottom of the paver chamfers) comply with this design guideline.
- Vertical changes in elevations among pavers do not exceed ¼ in. (6 mm). Changes between ¼ and ½ in. (6 and 13 mm) require a bevel and those over ½ in. (13 mm) require a ramp. PICP guide specification provided in Section 4 Construction limits vertical differences among pavers to ⅛ or 3 mm. Correctly installed concrete pavers have little or no vertical differences.

Figures 2-11. Various examples of pavement markings using PICP.

Pedestrian paths of travel through PICP parking lots should be studied and defined in the design stage. Vehicle lanes, parking spaces, pedestrian paths, and parking spaces for disabled persons can be delineated with different colored PICP or solid concrete pavers. See Figure 2-11. Likewise, parking spaces accessible to disabled persons can be paved with solid pavers and use a color contrasting with the PICP pavers.

Surface, Base/subbase and Soil Subgrade Infiltration Rates

PICP Surface Infiltration Rates—A common misunderstanding in PICP design is assuming that the percent of open surface area is equal to the percent of perviousness. For example, a 15% open PICP surface area is incorrectly assumed to be 15% pervious or 85% impervious. This suggests that 85% of the rain that falls on the PICP surface runs off which of course is not the case. All of the rain falling on the impervious paving units runs into the openings between them which makes their surface 100% pervious.

While PICP has less than 100% open surface area, the entire surface is considered 100% pervious since all water enters through it. Like all permeable pavements, water will not enter PICP if the surface is completely clogged with sediment. Avoiding this condition is covered in Section 5 Maintenance. The initial surface infiltration rate depends on the infiltration rates of joint filling material, bedding layer, and base/subbase materials, not the percentage of surface open area.

Initial surface infiltration rates on PICP are high. This is due to the joint filling material, typically ASTM No. 8, 89 or 9 stone. The permeability of ASTM No. 8 stone can exceed 2,000 in./hr (5,080 cm/hr)

and 89 and 9 stone often exceed 500 in./hr. (1,270 cm/hr) (NSA 1991). The US EPA measured surface infiltration rates (USEPA 2010) over the first six months of a PICP parking lot with ASTM No. 8 stone in the openings and bedding. Infiltration rates varied between 984 in./hr and 1,377 in./hr (2,500 and 3,500 cm/hr) using ASTM C 1701 (ASTM 2009), a single-ring infiltrometer test method.

Long-term Surface Infiltration Rates—There have been several other researchers who have investigated surface infiltration rates in new and older PICP. An extensive list follows. Bean (Bean 2007) found and average of 787 in/hr. (2,000 cm/hr) on nine parking lots in Maryland, Delaware and North Carolina using a single-ring infiltrometer. He also found significantly lower rates on PICP that received an extraordinary amount of fines deposited on the pavement surface. The most severely clogged surfaces showed infiltration rates similar to that of the soils in the openings, suggesting that some water may infiltrate if regular surface cleaning isn't conducted or if the surface is not exposed to traffic that might compact such soils on the surface. A low infiltration condition (i.e., below that of the design rainstorm intensity) from lack of routine cleaning can be restored to a higher infiltration rate. This process is covered in Section 5 Maintenance.

Studies by Beecham (Beecham 2009) in Australia also confirmed that continuously unmaintained PICP surfaces provide some infiltration. His research used a double-ring infiltrometer and measured between 0.5 and 37.5 in./hr (1.3 to 952 cm/hr) on unmaintained, eight- to just over ten-year old roads, parking lots and pedestrian areas in New South Wales and Victoria.

Collins (Collins 2007) measured surface infiltration rates on fairly new PICP test sites with 12.9% and 8.5% surface open areas using a double ring infiltrometer. Significantly higher infiltration rates were found on PICP with the higher percentage of open area. However, both PICP surfaces demonstrated 97% to 99% infiltration of rainfall from 40 events monitored.

In a laboratory study in Australia, Yong et al. (Yong 2008) compared surface and base infiltration rates of PICP and porous asphalt via accelerated simulation of over 17 years of stormwater for Melbourne and over 8 years for Brisbane. Selected PICP demonstrated no surface clogging after simulated polluted stormwater was poured onto these surfaces at rates equivalent to those periods for Brisbane and Melbourne. Total suspended solid removals were also high with lower nutrient reductions.

Shahin (Shahin 1994) constructed a laboratory installation of two PICP pavements (both with 12.2% open surface area), regular interlocking concrete pavers with sand jonts, impervious asphalt and examined pollutant reductions. The test apparatus enabled sloping of the installations up to 10% under a rainfall simulator. All pavements were tested with rainfall intensities up to 3.5 in./hr (90 mm/hr). While the study focused on pollutant reduction, Shahin's data indicates that at a 10% slope under 3.5 in./hr (90 mm/hr) of rainfall, approximately 2.5% of the rainfall converted to surface runoff on the two PICP surfaces tested. He observed that water ponding in joints and openings as the explanation for capturing rainfall and directing it inside the PICP. He also provides data that indicates little difference in water collected from the surface and subsurface when testing the two PICPs at 5% and 10% at a rainfall intensity of 3.5 in./hr (90 mm/hr).

Borgwardt (Borgwardt 1994, 1995, 1997, 2006) monitored infiltration rates of many new and older PICP in Germany and concluded that PICP surfaces loose 75% to 90% of their surface infiltration rate over the initial years of use. Infiltration rates then level off in the seventh or eighth year of service. This conclusion fits with broader experience with infiltration practices decreasing infiltration capacity over time due to sedimentation. This condition has been observed in pervious concrete (Chopra 2007) and porous asphalt (Ballestero 2009).

Borgwardt (Borgwardt 2006) found limited correlation between the surface infiltration performance and the percentage of paver surface open area. He could not find a strong relationship between actual infiltration performance and the percent of open area. Instead, he emphasized the selection of highly permeable aggregates for the joint filling as a more important consideration. Borgwardt also observed that smaller joint stone sizes render somewhat lower surface infiltration rates, but he noted that such

differences make little difference in the ability of the PICP surface to take in water. He notes that sand provides the lowest infiltration. For that reason, as well as its high clogging potential, ICPI recommends against using sand in PICP joints and the bedding layer.

Research, testing and experience have demonstrated that the key factors affecting surface infiltration are sediment deposition from traffic, soil eroding on the surface, and infrequent spills of topsoil or mulch. While the sources and amounts of sediment deposition will vary from site to site, the application of Borgwardt's suggested reductions (Borgwardt 2006) of initial surface infiltration of 75% to 90% still yields rates that will take in practically all storms. For example, if a PICP has an initial surface infiltration rate of 500 in./hour (1270 cm/hour) a 90% reduction over several years yields a surface infiltration rate 50 in./hr (127 cm/hr). *For design purposes, a conservative lowest surface infiltration for maintained PICP is 10 in./hour (25 cm/hour).*

Base/subbase infiltration—The initial and long-term infiltration rates of PICP base and subbase materials are very high, typically in the thousand of inches (cm) per hour. They are not considered an obstacle to water moving vertically through the pavement cross section. Designers may consider reduced flows from increasing levels or heads of water within a base as well as from horizontal movement of water through base and subbase materials. They will delay horizontal movement and the extensive amount of stone surfaces and mass help reduce flow rates. Models such as Darcy's Law to estimate horizontal flow rates and time of concentration within the stone materials are approximate.

More than surface infiltration, a key design consideration is the *lifetime* infiltration of soil subgrade. There can be short-term variations from a saturated soil subgrade and long-term reductions of infiltration from deposition of sediments. Studies by Gerrits (Gerrits 2002) and Bean (Bean 2007) demonstrated that much inbound sediment is trapped within the joints and bedding aggregates at the PICP surface. They also showed that removal of surface sediment increases surface infiltration rates. Sediment trapping and eventual removal (cleaning) helps slow the deposition of sediment onto the soil subgrade. However, deposition rates on the soil subgrade are almost impossible to predict. Therefore, a conservative approach should always be taken when establishing the design infiltration rate of the soil subgrade.

Figures 2-12 and 2-13. Upon plowing with standard plowing equipment, remaining snow can melt with water immediately entering the PICP surface. This reduces deicing and sand materials use as well as reducing liability hazards from slipping on ice.

Soil subgrade infiltration—ICPI recommends measuring the soil infiltration rate on the site and applying a safety factor of 2 for hydrologic design. For example, if the measured infiltration rate of a soil subgrade is 1 in./hr (25 mm/hr), then ½ in./hr (13 mm/hr) is the recommended design infiltration rate for calculations. This helps compensate for decreases in infiltration due to construction and sediment deposition over time. A higher factor of safety may be appropriate for sites with highly variable infiltration rates due to different soils or soil horizons. Recommended sampling and testing procedures for determining soil infiltration rates are provided on page 31.

Cold Climate Design Considerations

Experience with PICP in cold climates (e.g., Chicago and Toronto) has demonstrated no heaving after many winters. Should water freeze within an open-graded base, there is sufficient space between the aggregates to allow for water to expand (9%) as it freezes without their movement. Air in the spaces among aggregates and heat from the earth and water retained in the soil can extend thaw periods.

Research in Chicago, Illinois, further demonstrated the ability of the PICP base to not freeze in the winter. The City of Chicago Department of Transportation monitored ambient air and in the upper, middle, and lower portions Maxwell Street Market Plaza PICP parking lot from September 2008 to February 2009. Temperature data indicated that none of the PICP layers reached freezing temperatures. The coldest day, January 16, 2009, was -7° F (-21.7° C) not including the wind chill factor. The coldest Fahrenheit temperatures were as follows: upper area 33.4° (0.7° C) ; middle 34.1° (1.2° C) and lower base at 38.6° (3.7° C) (Attarian 2010).

Research on other permeable pavements in cold climates using open-graded bases (similar to that in PICP) provide further explanations for an absence of heaving and not needing a frost protection layer. Kevern (Kevern 2009) studied temperatures in open-graded bases under pervious concrete during the winter and concluded that, "Air in the aggregate base...acts as an insulating layer that, coupled with the higher latent heat associated with the higher soil moisture content, delays or eliminates the formation of a frost layer...while maintaining permeability." He also noted faster thawing than traditional concrete pavement.

Houle (Houle 2009) at the University of New Hampshire Stormwater Center measured air and base temperatures in an installation there of porous asphalt base. His findings agreed with Bäckström (Bäckström 2000) study on porous asphalt bases that yielded greater resistance to freezing, decreased frost penetration and more rapid thawing than conventional pavement due to higher water content in the underlying soil which increased the latent heat in the ground.

This heat-holding characteristic of open-graded bases enables permeable surfaces on them to use lower doses of deicing materials and commensurate cost savings. Substantial reductions have been observed on porous asphalt (UNHSC 2008) and PICP can expect similar reductions when sunlight exposure and temperatures melts snow and it immediately infiltrates into the surface. Figures 2-12 and 2-13 illustrate this melting which can also reduce slipping hazards from ice and related liability.

Unacceptably high concentrations of deicing salts and sand in snowmelt from impervious surfaces into PICP as well as those placed directly on it requires some design considerations. The considerations apply in climates with extended winters having large, rapid volumes of snow melt in the late winter and early spring. Such areas are mostly in the northern U.S. and Canada (Caraco 1997). There is no BMP including PICP that removes chlorides in deicing materials. Studies by Van Seters (2007) on PICP suggests that potential for deicing salts to mobilize heavy metals may warrant an increase in the depth of soil to the seasonally high ground water table 6.7 ft (2 m) or more below the PICP subbase for filtering purposes.

Sand applied for traction can reduce the surface infiltration rate of PICP surface and will require removal in the spring. Plowed and piled snow with chlorides and/or sand should be located on parking

lot islands or other vegetated areas. As an alternative to sand for traction, PICP joint filling stone can be used (i.e., ASTM No. 8, 9 or 89 stone). Maintenance should include annual inspection in the spring and vacuum removal of sand and surface sediment, as well as monitoring of groundwater for chlorides. This is paramount to continued infiltration performance and is covered in Section 5.

Managing salts and sand on a PICP site is a better option than collecting them on an impervious pavement and sending them in high concentrations to streams, lakes and rivers. If salts are used for deicing PICP and build up is a concern, then the soil and/or groundwater should be monitored. The amount of salts that locate in the soil and are transferred out of the PICP will vary and monitoring can be done through sampling water in observation wells located in the pavement base and soil. Chloride levels in the samples should be compared to local or national criteria for the particular use of the water in the receiving lake, stream, or river (e.g., drinking water, recreation, fishing, etc.).

If unacceptably high chloride concentrations in the runoff and groundwater are anticipated, then consideration should be given to using one or two design options below:

(a) Runoff from snowmelt can be diverted from the pavement during the winter. Diverting runoff away from the pavement is typically through pipes in base/subbase. Pipe valves must be operated each winter and spring. Snowmelt, however, cannot be treated but is diverted elsewhere.

(b) Oversized drainage pipes can be used to remove the runoff during snowmelt, and then be closed for the remainder of the year. The owner of the pavement must take responsibility for operating pipe valves that divert snowmelt. This may not be realistic with some designs.

When the local frost depth exceeds 3 ft (1 m), PICP should be set back from the subgrade of adjacent roads by at least 20 ft (6 m). This will reduce the potential for frost lenses and heaving of soil under the roadway. If this is not practical, another approach is using a vertical impermeable liner and perforated underdrains along the side of the PICP closest to a conventional roadbase to help block movement of water into the soil subgrade under the road.

Section 3. PICP Design

Desktop Assessment

A preliminary assessment is an essential prerequisite to detailed site, hydrological and structural design. This assessment includes a review of the following:

- Underlying geology and soils maps
- Identifying the NRCS hydrologic soil groups (A, B, C, D)
- Verifying history of fill soil, previous disturbances or compaction
- Review of topographical maps and identifying drainage patterns
- Identifying streams, wetlands, wells and structures
- Confirming absence of stormwater hotspots
- Identifying current and future land uses draining onto the site

PICP design involves structural and hydrological analyses as noted in Figure 3-1. PICP design merges these two previously disconnected spheres of civil engineering and design. The base/subbase thickness is determined for hydrological and structural (vehicular traffic loading) needs, and the thicker section is selected for drawings, specifications and construction. In many cases, the hydrologic requirements

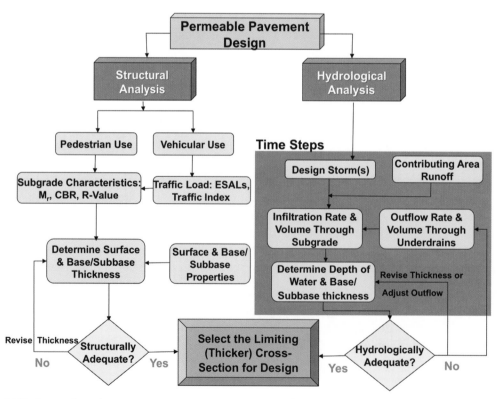

Figure 3-1. PICP design flow chart. See accompanying text that explains each step.

will require a thicker base than that required for supporting traffic. The following explains the design process by following the Figure 3-1 flow chart.

Structural Analysis

Traffic Load: ESALs, Traffic Index—This requires an estimate of the vehicular traffic loads expressed as 18,000 kip (80 kN) equivalent single axle loads (ESALs) or Caltrans Traffic Index (TI) over the design life of the pavement, typically 20 years. The ESAL concept recognizes that when a vehicle passes over a pavement, it damages it. The cumulative effects of many passes (ESALs) eventually causes ruts or cracks making the pavement unserviceable and needing rehabilitation.

Vehicles passing over a pavement exert a wide range of axle loads. Compared to automobiles, trucks and busses do the most damage to pavements because their loads are much higher than automobiles. One pass of a fully loaded truck will do more damage to pavement than several thousand automobiles passing over it.

The 18,000 lb (80 kN) emerged as a convenient basis for characterizing loads from trucks as part of the American Association of State Highway and Transportation Officials (AASHTO) road tests conducted in the 1950s. The number of ESALs is determined by the weight of each axle and dividing them by a standard ESAL of 18,000 lbs or 80 kN. For example, a five axle trailer-truck has two rear axles on the trailer each exerting 18,000 lbs (80 kN); two on the back of the truck at 15,800 lbs (70 kN); and one in the front (steering) of the truck at 11,000 lbs (50 kN).

AASHTO uses "load equivalency factors" or LEFs for each axle to estimate ESALs from vehicles. LEFs and resulting ESALs for one pass of this truck over a pavement are calculated as follows (in kN):

Trailer: $(80/80)^4$ = 1 (x 2 axles) = 2 ESALs
Truck rear: $(70/80)^4$ = 0.6 (x 2 axles) = 1.2 ESALs
Truck front: $(50/80)^4$ = 0.15 ESALs
When added together LEFs = 2 + 1.2 = 0.15 = 3.35 ESALs.

In other words, for every pass across a pavement, the trailer-truck exerts 3.35 18,000 lbs (80 kN) ESALs. ESALs are estimated for a range of truck configurations expected to use a pavement over its lifetime. To put automobile axle loads into perspective, the two axle loads from one passenger automobile placed into the formula yields about 0.0002 ESALs. Therefore, pavement design primarily considers trucks because they exert the highest loads and most damage. In contrast, thousands of automobiles are required to apply the same loading and damage as one passage of a truck. Since PICP is designed mostly for parking lots and residential roads, total lifetime ESALs are typically less than 600,000 ESALs. Even at this level of lifetime ESALs, PICP can withstand a significant amount of axle loads from trucks. This has been verified with PICP used in fire stations and commercial parking lots that experience truck traffic.

PICP can support an AASHTO H-20 truck load. This characterization of one truck axle loading was developed for bridge design. AASHTO H-20 loading is defined in the AASHTO publication, *Standard Specifications for Highway Bridges* and is one front axle load of 8,000 lbs (36 kN) and a single rear axle (tandem wheels) of 32,000 lbs (142 kN). H-20 loading is mistakenly construed as a basis for pavement design which typically characterizes ESALs as 18,000 lb (80 kN) repetitions and not as a single load. H-20 loads will require characterization as repetitions in order to be used in pavement design.

Subgrade Characteristics: M_r, CBR, R-value—Soil stability under traffic should be carefully reviewed for each application by a qualified geotechnical or civil engineer and lowest anticipated soil strength or stiffness values used for design. The structural design procedure explained below relies on soil characterized using resilient modulus (M_r), California Bearing Ratio (CBR), or resistance (R-value). Correlations among M_r, CBR and R-value are provided in *ICPI Tech Spec 4–Structural Design of Interlocking Concrete Pavements*. Transportation agencies and design engineers use one or more of these to characterize the ability of soil to withstand traffic loads.

PICP structural design for vehicular applications assumes a minimum soil CBR (96-hour soaked per ASTM D 1883 or AASHTO T 193) of 4%, or a minimum R-value = 9 per ASTM D 2844 or AASHTO T-190, or a minimum M_r of 6,500 psi (45 MPa) per AASHTO T-307 to qualify for use under vehicular traffic. Soil compaction required to achieve this will reduce the infiltration rate of the soil. Therefore, the permeability or infiltration rate of soil should be assessed at the density required to achieve at least 4% soaked CBR. Pedestrian applications can be placed on lower strength soils.

If soils have a soaked CBR<4% or are expansive when wet, one option is treatment to raise the CBR above 4% and stabilize them. Treatment can be with cement, lime or lime/flyash. Guidelines on the amount and depth of cement required for soil stabilization can be found in publications by the Portland Cement Association (PCA 2003). Soil stabilization will render essentially no infiltration and this should be reflected in the hydrologic analysis. Cement- or asphalt-stablized base/subbase aggregates are another option. This is covered below under "Base/subbase Properties."

Structural Design Methods—For structural design of impervious (conventional) roads and base, as well as interlocking concrete pavements, many local, state and provincial agencies use design methods published by AASHTO. While the AASHTO flexible pavement design methodology is familiar to many civil engineers, stormwater agency personnel who do not deal with pavement design are encouraged to become familiar with and reference it in PICP recommendations for local, state or provincial BMP and LID manuals, and regulatory documents.

Highway engineers increasingly use AASHTO *Guide for Mechanistic-Empirical Design of New and Rehabilitated Pavement Structures* (AASHTO 2004) which relies on mechanistic design and modeling, i.e., analysis of loads and resultant stresses and strains on materials and the soil subgrade. The AASHTO mechanistic design model was developed and calibrated by state, provincial and federal highway agencies using a wide range of highway loads, soil types and climatic conditions. ICPI is working with these same agencies to calibrate the model for PICP applications specifically for open-graded, crushed stone bases.

Many local transportation agencies use the empirically-based AASHTO 1993 *Guide for Design of Pavement Structures* (AASHTO 1993) to determine pavement cross sections. The concepts in the *Guide* emerged from tests in the 1950s that established relationships among materials types, loads and serviceability. The AASHTO design equation in the 1993 *Guide* calculates a structural number or SN given traffic loads (ESALs), soil type, climatic and moisture conditions. The designer then finds the appropriate combination of pavement surfacing and base materials to meet or exceed the required SN. Values for SNs range between 2 for local roads to as high as 10 for highways.

Load distribution and transfer of loads through the surface and base in PICP is similar to flexible pavement with consideration to the stress-dependent nature of the base/subbase aggregates. Therefore, PICP can be characterized as a flexible pavement system and 1993 AASHTO design method can be applied to it (Swan 2009) with some adaptations. A key input for flexible pavement design to meet or exceed a given design SN is the "layer coefficient" which characterizes the stiffness of each pavement layer with a number; the higher the coefficient, the stiffer the material. The coefficient is expressed per inch or per 25 millimeters of pavement layer thickness. The thickness of each pavement material is multiplied by the layer coefficients and all coefficients are added to equal or exceed the required SN.

For example, given site specific inputs on subgrade soil strength, climate, moisture and traffic loads, the AASHTO flexible pavement design equation yields a required structural number of 3 for a local road. The designer then identifies the combination of pavement layer materials whose layer coefficients total at least 3. In this illustration, a compacted, dense-graded crushed stone base typically has a layer coefficient of 0.14 per inch or 25 mm of thickness. Standard interlocking concrete pavers at 3 1/8 in. (80 mm) thickness and 1 in. (25 mm) of bedding sand typically have a layer coefficient of 0.44 per inch (ASCE 2010). Therefore, the 4 1/8 in. (105 mm) thick paver and sand layer provides a SN of 0.44 x 4.15 = 1.82. The base layer thickness required would then be 3 – 1.82 = 1.18/0.14 = 8.4 or about 9 in. (225 mm). The paver bedding sand and base layer coefficients together satisfy the required structural number.

Base/subbase Properties—Dense-graded road base consists of crushed stone and fines (material passing the No. 100 and 200 or 0.150 and 0.075 mm sieves) with densities from approximately 120 to 145 pcf (1,922 to 2,322 kg/m³) with porosities less than 15%. In contrast, open-graded bases for PICP have no fines (≤2% passing the No. 200 sieve) and are typically 95 to 120 pcf (1,522 to 1,922 kg/m³). Porosities exceed 30% for water storage. Porosity is the volume of voids divided by the total volume of the base.

Jointing, bedding, base and subbase aggregates used in vehicular PICP applications should be crushed with minimum 90% fractured faces and a minimum Los Angeles (LA) abrasion <40 per ASTM C131 and C535. For base/subbase materials, a minimum porosity of 0.32 and CBR of at least 80% are recommended. Porosity can be approximated using ASTM C 29. Sieve analysis of washed gradations should be per ASTM C 136.

The layer coefficients of dense-graded road bases generally range from 0.10 to 0.14 per inch or 25 mm of material thickness, or a resilient modulus of 13,500 to about 20,000 psi (93 to 138 MPa). The layer coefficients of open-graded crushed stone bases such as ASTM No. 57 and ASTM No. 2 stone are not as well researched (with accelerated loading and modeling) or their behavior as well understood as dense-graded bases. This will likely change over time with the advent of permeable pavements.

Layer coefficients for open-graded materials in PICP are generally recognized as being lower than that for dense-graded materials. In addition, PICP design conditions must consider an intentionally saturated base/subbase and soil subgrade. Shackel (2006) suggests open-graded base resilient modulus between 36,260 and 58,000 psi (250 and 400 MPa) but qualifies them with reductions between 40% and 70% due to saturation and stress dependency (i.e., base stiffness depends on applied loads).

Jones (2010) notes that, "...an open-graded base course is used to maximize water storage. This influences the degree of compaction and resultant strength that can be achieved. The base course will therefore typically need to be thicker to compensate for the lower strengths and stiffnesses associated with the less dense grading." Jones conducted laboratory resilient modulus testing on four open-graded base materials from quarries in northern California using AASHTO T-307 and measured ranges between 110 to 400 MPa (16,000 to 58,000 psi) over increasing bulk stresses. There is no information on the moisture of the tested aggregates. The results "indicated little difference in performance between the three material types, although the finer (fourth material), more graded samples had a slightly higher resilient modulus, as expected. The resilient modulus values were considerably lower than those typically obtained from testing conventional dense-graded aggregate base course materials."

Other researchers have characterized the structural capacity of open-graded bases. Raad (Raad 1994) compared laboratory resilient modulus of non-saturated ASTM No. 57 stone at 18,000 psi (124 MPa) to typical dense-graded road base at 26,000 psi (179 MPa), an increase of about 44%. Raad also found that ASTM No. 57 stone remained more stable in saturated conditions by avoiding pore pressures from water common to dense-graded bases with material passing the No. 200 (0.075) sieve. This finding suggests that open-graded bases can remain stable in saturated (generally worst case) conditions. Such stability under loads ultimately depends on the stability of a continuously saturated soil subgrade, the worst case design scenario.

Hein (Hein 2006) also conducted laboratory resilient modulus testing of open-graded bases using AASHTO T-307 and obtained stiffness similar to that from testing a dense-graded base. Bases were not tested in a saturated condition so lower values might be expected for design purposes. Salem (Salem 2006) found that a gradation similar to ASTM No. 3 stone drainage layer consistently provided greater subbase structural support in non-saturated conditions under a typical state DOT dense-graded road base than pavements without the ASTM No. 3 stone.

Some state transportation agencies specify well-graded aggregates as permeable bases (drainage layers) under conventional pavements (either unstabilized, or stabilized with asphalt or cement). These same aggregates can be used in PICP as long as they meet certain gradations, and only under certain

conditions, as detailed below. In terms of gradation, these bases can have a higher percentage of material passing the No. 4 (4.75 mm) sieve than those described in this manual, but are limited to 2% passing the No. 200 (0.075 mm) sieve. Using such bases for PICP can be a design option when water storage is not the primary objective, for example, when smaller rainfall depths are captured, treated and released. Stability is increased by using underdrains that prevent saturation of the aggregates, and related pore pressures. Such underdrains are recommended in all applications to prevent this condition. Consultation with an experienced pavement engineer is recommended regarding assessment of the structural contribution of such bases especially when stabilized with asphalt or cement. Other aggregate bases may also be used if they are deemed to meet the hydrological and structural requirements of the projects by the engineer/designer of record.

Transportation agencies often have specifications for stabilized open-graded bases using cement or asphalt. Stabilized bases including pervious concrete can be used to increase the base stiffness and strength over weak soils. For the purposes of this manual, only non-stabilized bases and subbases design is covered. Experience with using stabilized bases or subbase in PICP for high ESAL applications (i.e. over 1 million ESALs) is limited and requires expertise of an experienced pavement engineer.

Surface Structural Contribution—Many accelerated traffic studies and non-destructive testing have defined the layer coefficient of (non-permeable) interlocking concrete pavements and the bedding sand layer equal to or higher than an equivalent thickness of asphalt, typically 0.44 per inch (or 25 mm) of thickness. Many of these studies are summarized in a report by Rollings (Rollings 1992). Some studies have measured AASHTO layer coefficients higher than 0.44 due to progressive stiffening of the paver and bedding sand layers.

In contrast, testing to characterize the layer coefficient of the pavers and bedding in PICP has been minimal. PICP layer coefficients are estimated between 0.20 to 0.40 with 0.3 as an average value. This value includes a $3^{1}/8$ in. (80 mm) thick filled with ASTM No. 8, 9 or 89 stone, and a 2 in. (50 mm) thick bedding layer of typical ASTM No. 8 bedding stone directly under PICP units. This value considers wider joints in PICP and filled with aggregate with a lower contact area with the adjacent paver sides than those in interlocking concrete pavement with sand-filled joints. Manufacturers of pavers used in PICP may have additional information and test results that characterize the layer coefficient for their pavers, using specific jointing and bedding materials. They may also have additional information that characterizes benefits of specific paver shapes on structural and hydrologic design, installation and maintenance.

Determine Surface and Base/Subbase Thickness—PICP surfaces for vehicular traffic are typically $3^{1}/8$ in. (80 mm) thick over 2 in. (50 mm) layer of ASTM No. 8 stone. Moving on to base/subbase thicknesses, German PICP design guidelines (Zement 2003) recommend a minimum resilient modulus for base materials at 14,500 psi (100 MPa). This design value is on the low (conservative) side for PICP base materials. The German guidelines recommend a minimum soil subgrade M_r = 6,500 psi or 45 MPa (i.e., CBR 4.3%). Consistent with this conservative design approach, Table 3-1 provides recommended PICP structural design using the 1993 AASHTO design method for flexible pavements. All bases for vehicular traffic are 4 in. (100 mm) thick ASTM No. 57 stone. The table provides subbase thickness solutions using ASTM No. 2 stone given ESALs or TIs and soil characterizations. ASTM No. 3 or 4 stone subbases are applicable.

The layer thicknesses in Table 3-1 are designed with the following assumptions: 80% confidence level; commercial vehicles = 10% in the traffic mix; and the average ESALs per commercial vehicle = 2. Conservative layer coefficients are used for the base and subbase where the ASTM No. 57 stone base = 0.09; ASTM No. 2 stone layer coefficient = 0.06. These approximate resilient modulus values of 19,300 and 12,800 psi (133 and 88 MPa) respectively. Experience has shown that a frost protection layer of additional base is not required provided that the soil subgrade drains water prior to freezing and/or through perforated pipes. The minimal fines in the base and subbase help prevent accumulation of water that would create frost heaving.

Pedestrian applications use only the ASTM No. 57 stone base with a minimum thickness of 6 in. (150 mm). Thicker bases can be used for additional water storage. Residential driveways have a minimum 6 in. (150 mm) ASTM No. 2 subbase over a 4 in. (100 mm) thick ASTM No. 57 base. Some designs may use ASTM No. 57 stone for the entire driveway base and subbase.

Hydrological Analysis

Design Storm—The design storm(s) with the return period and intensity in inches or millimeters per hour is typically supplied by the municipality or other regulatory agency. Rainfall intensity-duration-frequency maps or databases can be referenced to establish the design storm for the eastern half of the U.S. (Hershfield 1961), western half (west of the 105th meridian) (Miller 1973), or Canada (Environment Canada 2010).

Contributing Area Runoff—Some PICP design may receive runoff from roofs, adjacent impervious pavement and pervious areas. The total area and contributing runoff from it should be estimated using the design storm(s) if applicable. The total impervious area draining into the PICP should not exceed five times the area of the PICP. This recognizes that a typical design situation can be a site with runoff from roofs and impervious pavement for parking or roads that drains into PICP. The movement of water from impervious pavements into PICP is typically designed as sheet flow. The inlet capacity of PICP is assumed to be infinite and is not a design factor.

Infiltration Rate & Volume Through the Subgrade—Subsequent to the desktop assessment is a more in-depth investigation of the site. This includes tests for soil infiltration that inform a decision on the design soil infiltration rate. The soil sampling and testing should be designed and supervised by a licensed professional (geotechnical or civil) engineer knowledgeable of local soils. Besides infiltration test results, this engineer should provide a soils report that includes assessment of design strength, compaction requirements as needed and other appropriate site assessment information. Some guidelines follow on sampling and testing procedures to help determine the design soil infiltration rate.

Test pits dug with a backhoe are recommended for every 7,000 sf (700 m²) of paving with a minimum of two holes per site. All pits should be dug at least 5 ft (1.5 m) deep with soil logs recorded to at least 3 ft (1 m) below the bottom of the base. More test pits at various depths (horizons) may be required by the engineer in areas where soil types may change, near rock outcroppings, in low lying areas or where the water table is likely to be within 6 ft (1.8 m) of the surface. Evidence of a high water table, impermeable soil layers, rock or dissimilar layers may require a no exfiltration design.

The following tests are recommended on soils from the test pit, especially if the soil has clay content. Besides assessing infiltration potential, the tests can assist in evaluating the soil's suitability for supporting traffic in a saturated condition. Other tests may be required by the design engineer. AASHTO tests equivalent to ASTM methods may be used.

1. Unified (USCS) soil classification per ASTM D 2487.

Caution: Laboratory infiltration (permeability) tests are not recommended as soil samples have a high risk of structure and porosity changes. Results from field tests can be better approximations because the structure and porosity of soils are not as easily changed. However, caution is still required in conducting field tests on least disturbed soil as a result of excavation. On-site tests do not account for loss of the soil's conductivity from construction, compaction and clogging from sediment. Nor do they account for lateral drainage of water from the soil into the sides of the base. Individual test results should not be considered absolute values directly representative of expected drawdown of water from the open-graded base. Instead, the test results should be interpreted with permeability estimates based on soil texture, structure, pore geometry and consistence (Fairfax 1991). As previously noted, for design purposes, a factor of safety of 2 should be applied to the average or typical measured site soil infiltration rate.

2. Sampled moisture content in percent.

3. Onsite tests of the infiltration rate of the soil. Use local, state or provincial recommendations for test methods and frequency if they exist. All tests for infiltration should be done at the approximate elevation corresponding to the bottom of the subbase and in a saturated state. If there are no requirements for infiltration test methods, ASTM D 3385 *Test Method for Infiltration Rate of Soils in Field Using a Double-Ring Infiltrometer* is recommended. ASTM D 5093 *Test Method for Field Measurement of Infiltration Rate Using a Double-Ring Infiltrometer with a sealed Inner Ring* is for

Table 3-1. Recommended minimum PICP subbase & base thicknesses

PEDESTRIAN	Soaked CBR (R-value)	4 (9)	5 (11)	6 (12.5)	7 (14)	8 (15.5)	9 (17)	10 (18)
	Resilient Modulus, psi (MPa)*	6,205 (43)	7,157 (49)	8,043 (55)	8,877 (61)	9,669 (67)	10,426 (72)	11,153 (77)
	Base thickness, in. (mm) ASTM No. 57	6 (150)						

VEHICULAR	Soaked CBR (R-value)	4 (9)	5 (11)	6 (12.5)	7 (14)	8 (15.5)	9 (17)	10 (18)
	Resilient Modulus, psi (MPa)*	6,205 (43)	7,157 (49)	8,043 (55)	8,877 (61)	9,669 (67)	10,426 (72)	11,153 (77)
Lifetime ESALs (Traffic Index)								
50,000 (6.3) and Residential Driveways	Base thickness, in. (mm) ASTM No. 57	4 (100)						
	Subbase thickness in. (mm) ASTM No. 2	6 (150)						
100,000 (6.8)	Base thickness, in. (mm) ASTM No. 57	4 (100)						
	Subbase thickness in. (mm) ASTM No. 2	8 (200)	6 (150)					
200,000 (7.4)	Base thickness, in. (mm) ASTM No. 57	4 (100)	4 (100)					
	Subbase thickness in. (mm) ASTM No. 2	13 (325)	11 (275)	9 (225)	7 (175)	6 (150)		
300,000 (7.8)	Base thickness, in. (mm) ASTM No. 57	4 (100)	4 (100)	4 (100)	4 (100)	4 (100)		
	Subbase thickness in. (mm) ASTM No. 2	16 (400)	14 (350)	12 (300)	10 (250)	9 (225)	8 (200)	7 (175)
400,000 (8.1)	Base thickness, in. (mm) ASTM No. 57	4 (100)	4 (100)	4 (100)	4 (100)	4 (100)	4 (100)	4 (100)
	Subbase thickness in. (mm) ASTM No. 2	19 (475)	16 (400)	14 (350)	12 (300)	11 (275)	10 (250)	9 (225)
500,000 (8.3)	Base thickness, in. (mm) ASTM No. 57	4 (100)	4 (100)	4 (100)	4 (100)	4 (100)	4 (100)	4 (100)
	Subbase thickness in. (mm) ASTM No. 2	21 (525)	18 (450)	16 (400)	14 (350)	12 (300)	11 (275)	10 (250)
600,000 (8.5)	Base thickness, in. (mm) ASTM No. 57	4 (100)	4 (100)	4 (100)	4 (100)	4 (100)	4 (100)	4 (100)
	Subbase thickness in. (mm) ASTM No. 2	22 (550)	19 (475)	17 (425)	15 (375)	14 (350)	12 (300)	11 (275)
700,000 (8.6)	Base thickness, in. (mm) ASTM No. 57	4 (100)	4 (100)	4 (100)	4 (100)	4 (100)	4 (100)	4 (100)
	Subbase thickness in. (mm) ASTM No. 2	24 (600)	21 (525)	18 (450)	17 (425)	15 (375)	14 (350)	12 (300)
800,000 (8.8)	Base thickness, in. (mm) ASTM No. 57	4 (100)	4 (100)	4 (100)	4 (100)	4 (100)	4 (100)	4 (100)
	Subbase thickness in. (mm) ASTM No. 2	25 (625)	22 (550)	20 (500)	18 (450)	16 (400)	15 (375)	13 (325)
900,000 (8.9)	Base thickness, in. (mm) ASTM No. 57	4 (100)	4 (100)	4 (100)	4 (100)	4 (100)	4 (100)	4 (100)
	Subbase thickness in. (mm) ASTM No. 2	26 (650)	23 (575)	21 (525)	19 (475)	17 (425)	16 (400)	14 (350)
1,000,000 (9)	Base thickness, in. (mm) ASTM No. 57	4 (100)	4 (100)	4 (100)	4 (100)	4 (100)	4 (100)	4 (100)
	Subbase thickness in. (mm) ASTM No. 2	27 (675)	24 (600)	21 (525)	19 (475)	18 (425)	16 (400)	15 (375)

*M_r in psi = 2,555 x $CBR^{0.64}$; M_r in MPa = 17.61 x $CBR^{0.64}$
Assumptions: 80% confidence level
Commercial vehicles = 10%; Average ESALs per commercial vehicle = 2
ASTM No. 57 stone layer coefficient = 0.09; ASTM No. 2 stone layer coefficient = 0.06
ASTM No. 3 or 4 stone may be substituted for ASTM No. 2 stone subbase layer.
$3^1/8$ in. (80 mm) thick concrete pavers and 2 in. (50 mm) ASTM No. 8 bedding layer coefficient = 0.3
Total PICP cross section depth equals the sum of the subbase, base, 2 in. (50 mm) bedding and paver $3^1/8$ in. (80 mm) thickness.
Consult with geogrid manufacturers for base/subbase thickness recommendations using geogrids.

Table 3-2. Suitability of soils (per the Unified Soils Classification System) for infiltration of stormwater and bearing capacity (Cao 1998). This table provides general guidance. Testing and evaluation of soils are highly recommended.

USCS Soil Classification	Typical ranges for Coefficient of Permeability, k, in./hour (approximate m/s)	Relative Permeability when compacted and saturated	Shearing strength when compacted	Compressibility	Typical CBR Range
GW-well graded gravels	1.3 to 137 (10^{-5} to 10^{-3})	Pervious	Excellent	Negligible	30-80
GP-poorly graded gravels	6.8 to 137 (5×10^{-5} to 10^{-3})	Very pervious	Good	Negligible	20-60
GM-silty gravels	1.3×10^{-4} to 13.5 (10^{-8} to 10^{-4})	Semi-pervious to impervious	Good	Negligible	20-60
GC-clayey gravel	1.3×10^{-4} to 1.3×10^{-2} (10^{-8} to 10^{-6})	Impervious	Good to fair	Very low	20-40
SW-well graded sands	0.7 to 68 (5×10^{-6} to 5×10^{-4})	Pervious	Excellent	Negligible	10-40
SP-poorly graded sands	0.07 to 0.7 (5×10^{-7} to 5×10^{-6})	Pervious to semi-pervious	Good	Very low	10-40
SM-silty sands	1.3×10^{-4} to 0.7 (10^{-9} to 5×10^{-6})	Semi-pervious to impervious	Good	Low	10-40
SC-clayey sands	1.3×10^{-5} to 0.7 (10^{-9} to 5×10^{-6})	Impervious	Good to fair	Low	5-20
ML-inorganic silts of low plasticity	1.3×10^{-5} to 0.07 (10^{-9} to 5×10^{-7})	Impervious	Fair	Medium	2-15
CL-inorganic clays of low plasticity	1.3×10^{-5} to 1.3×10^{-3} (10^{-9} to 10^{-8})	Impervious	Fair	Medium	2-5
OL-organic silts of low plasticity	1.3×10^{-5} to 1.3×10^{-2} (10^{-9} to 10^{-6})	Impervious	Poor	Medium	2-5
MH-inorganic silts of high plasticity	1.3×10^{-6} to 1.3×10^{-5} (10^{-10} to 10^{-9})	Very impervious	Fair to poor	High	2-10
CH-inorganic clays of high plasticity	1.3×10^{-7} to 1.3×10^{-5} (10^{-11} to 10^{-9})	Very impervious	Poor	High	2-5
OH-organic clays of high plasticity	Not appropriate under permeable interlocking concrete pavements				
PT-Peat, mulch, soils with high organic content	Not appropriate under permeable interlocking concrete pavements				

soils with an expected infiltration rate of 1.4×10^{-2} in./hr (10^{-7} cm/sec) to 1.4×10^{-5} in./hr (10^{-9} cm/sec). Portable infiltration devices have been successfully used to help assess a design soil subgrade infiltration rates for permeable pavements (Turf-Tec 2007). While informative for obtaining initial estimates, percolation test results for the design of septic drain fields are not recommended for the design of stormwater infiltration systems as they can overestimate soil infiltration rates (Fairfax 1991) (Oram 2003).

Table 3-2 provides some guidance on the permeability and range of California Bearing Ratio (CBR) strengths for soils classified using the Unified Soils Classification System (USCS). Soils with a tested permeability equal to or greater than 0.5 in./hr (3.5×10^{-4} m/sec) usually will be gravel, sand, loamy sand, sandy loam, loam, and silt loam. These are usually soils with no more than 10-12% passing the No. 200 (0.075 mm) sieve.

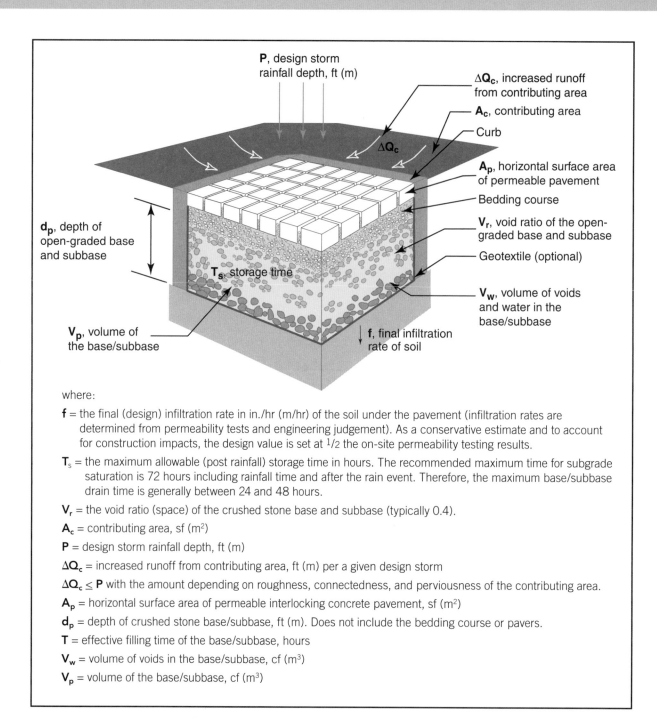

where:

f = the final (design) infiltration rate in in./hr (m/hr) of the soil under the pavement (infiltration rates are determined from permeability tests and engineering judgement). As a conservative estimate and to account for construction impacts, the design value is set at $1/2$ the on-site permeability testing results.

T$_s$ = the maximum allowable (post rainfall) storage time in hours. The recommended maximum time for subgrade saturation is 72 hours including rainfall time and after the rain event. Therefore, the maximum base/subbase drain time is generally between 24 and 48 hours.

V$_r$ = the void ratio (space) of the crushed stone base and subbase (typically 0.4).

A$_c$ = contributing area, sf (m^2)

P = design storm rainfall depth, ft (m)

ΔQ$_c$ = increased runoff from contributing area, ft (m) per a given design storm

ΔQ$_c$ ≤ P with the amount depending on roughness, connectedness, and perviousness of the contributing area.

A$_p$ = horizontal surface area of permeable interlocking concrete pavement, sf (m^2)

d$_p$ = depth of crushed stone base/subbase, ft (m). Does not include the bedding course or pavers.

T = effective filling time of the base/subbase, hours

V$_w$ = volume of voids in the base/subbase, cf (m^3)

V$_p$ = volume of the base/subbase, cf (m^3)

Figure 3-2. Design Parameters for calculating the base depth for PICP full exfiltration systems.

On-site soil infiltration testing is expensive and residential and some commercial PICP projects may not justify the expense. In such cases, a soil classification can be used to estimate permeability by selecting conservative (lower) values from the ranges provided in Table 3-2. Another method is using the NRCS hydrologic soil groups (HSG) A, B, C or D which characterize the saturated conductivity according to sand, silt or clay content, the depth to the impermeable layer and the depth to high water table (USDA 2003). Chapter 7 Hydrologic Soil Groups of the aforementioned reference issued in 2009 (available on-line) provides estimated ranges of saturated conductivity for the four groups. Again, conservative values should be selected from this reference for estimating soil subgrade permeability. Silt and clay soils with lower permeability often require perforated drain pipes per a partial exfiltration design. These are typically NCRS type C and D soils.

Determine Water Depth and Base/subbase Thickness—The following procedure is for sizing the base/subbase for full exfiltration designs, i.e., no underdrains. Figure 3-2 provides a summary of symbols used in PICP calculations.

To ensure that the subgrade does not remain saturated for longer than the maximum allowable storage time (T_s), the maximum allowable base/subbase depth (d_{max}) in feet (m) needs to be determined, the following equation is used to calculate d_{max}:

$$d_{max} = f \times T_s / V_r \qquad \text{(Equation 1)}$$

The design volume of water to be stored in the pavement base (V_w) is:

the runoff volume from the adjacent contributing area;	plus	the rainfall volume falling on the permeable pavement	minus	the exfiltration volume into the underlying soil
$= \Delta Q_c A_c$	$+$	PA_p	$-$	fTA_p

As the effective filling time of the base/subbase (**T**) cannot be calculated without first knowing the depth of the base/subbase (d_p), it is necessary to make an assumption of **T**. For designs based on NRCS Type II, the permeable pavement base/subbase filling time is generally less than a 2-hour duration where the flow into the pavement exceeds the flow out of the pavement. An NRCS Type II storm represents the most intense, short duration, and most common within the continental U.S. among the storm types defined by NRCS. Thus, a duration of 2 hours is used in the equations below. This value of course should be adjusted by the designer to reflect the local design storm.

The volume of the stone base and subbase (V_p) can also be defined in terms of its geometry:

$$V_p = V_w/V_r = d_p A_p$$

Setting the previous two equations equal will result in the following relationship:

$$d_p A_p V_r = \Delta Q_c A_c + PA_p - fTA_P \qquad \text{(Equation 2)}$$

The surface area of the permeable pavement (A_p) and the depth of the base (d_p) can be defined in the following forms from the above equation:

$$A_p = \frac{\Delta Q_c A_c}{V_r d_p - P + fT} \qquad \text{(Equation 3)}$$

and

$$d_p = \frac{\Delta Q_c R + P - fT}{V_r} \qquad \text{(Equation 4)}$$

Where:

R = equal to the ratio of the contributing area and the permeable pavement area (A_c/A_p).

Design Procedure—There are two methods to calculate the required base/subbase dimensions. The first method computes the minimum depth of the base, given the area of the permeable pavement. This is called the *minimum depth method*. The other computes the minimum surface area of the permeable pavement given the required design depth of the base. This is the *minimum area method*. The minimum depth method generally will be more frequently used since the surface area is typically known while the depth of the stone base/subbase is to be determined.

Minimum Depth Method

1. From the selected design rainfall (**P**) compute the increased runoff volume from the contributing area ($\Delta\mathbf{Q_c}$).

2. Compute the depth of the aggregate base (**d$_p$**) from Equation 4:

3. Compute the maximum allowable depth (**d$_{max}$**) of the aggregate base and subbase using Equation 1:

$$\mathbf{d_{max} = f \times T_s / V_r}$$

where **d$_p$** must be less than or equal to **d$_{max}$** and at least 2 feet (0.6 m) above the seasonal high ground water table. If **d$_p$** does not satisfy this criteria, the surface area of the permeable pavement must be increased or a smaller design storm must be selected. Another option is using drain pipes to create a partial exfiltration system.

Minimum Area Method

1. From the selected design rainfall (**P**) and the contributing area to be drained, compute the increased runoff depth from the contributing area ($\Delta\mathbf{Q_c}$).

2. Compute the maximum allowable depth (**d$_{max}$**) of the aggregate base/subbase from Equation 1:

$$\mathbf{d_{max} = f \times T_s / V_r}$$

Select a design depth of the aggregate base (**d$_p$**) less than or equal to **d$_{max}$** or the depth at least 2 feet (0.6 m) above the seasonal high ground water table, whichever is smaller.

3. Compute the minimum required PICP surface area (**A$_p$**) from Equation 3:

$$\mathbf{A_p = \frac{\Delta Q_c \, A_c.}{V_r d_p - P \times fT}}$$

Sizing Example—Full Exfiltration

Step 1—Assess site conditions. A parking lot in Durham, New Hampshire is being designed in an urbanized area where storm sewers have limited capacity to convey runoff from an increase in existing impervious surfaces. Runoff from a 2 acre (8,094 m^2) asphalt parking lot (assume 100% imperviousness) is to be captured by a 1 acre (4,047 m^2) PICP area over an open-graded base (**R** = 2). Since the area is known, the minimum depth method is used. The project is not close to building foundations nor are there any wells in the area.

Soil borings revealed that the seasonal high water is 10 ft (3 m) below grade. The soil borings and testing indicated a USCS classification of GM (silty gravel) with 18% passing the No. 200 (0.075 mm) sieve. Infiltration was field tested at 4.8 in./hr (0.4 ft/hr or 3.4 x 10^{-5} m/sec). While this was the tested rate, the designer is taking a conservative position on design infiltration by assuming it at half or **f** = 2.4 in./hr (0.2 ft/hr or 1.7 x 10^{-5} m/sec). This approach recognizes a loss of permeability from construction, soil compaction and soil subgrade clogging over time. The 96-hour soaked CBR of the soil is 6%. An estimated 600,000 ESALs will traffic this parking lot over 20 years.

Local regulations require this site to capture and when possible infiltrate all rainfall and runoff from a 2-year 24 hour storm which is 3 in. (0.25 ft or 0.076 m) based on rainfall maps. The void space in the ASTM No. 57 open-graded, crushed stone base and ASTM No. 2 subbase provided by the local quarry are 40% or 0.40. A two-day drainage of the base/subbase (or 48-hour drawdown) is a design criterion. Since the PICP parking lot area is established at one acre, the depth of the base needs to be determined with the Minimum Depth Method.

Step 2—Compute the increased runoff depth from the contributing area ($\Delta\mathbf{Q_c}$) from the selected design rainfall (**P**) Since the contributing area is impervious asphalt, all of the rainfall being 3 in. (0.25 ft or

0.076 m) will flow from it into the PICP. The impervious area is less than five times the area of the PICP.

Step 3—Compute the depth of the aggregate base/subbase (d_p) from Equation 4:

$$d_p = \frac{\Delta Q_c\, R + P\text{-}fT}{V_r} = \frac{0.25 \text{ ft (2 ac./1 ac.)} + 0.25 \text{ ft} - 0.2 \text{ ft/hr (2 hr)}}{0.4}$$

d_p = 0.875 ft (10.5 in. or 0.26 m) This thickness represents the total ASTM No. 57 stone base (4 in. or 100 mm thick) plus the ASTM No. 2 stone subbase thickness.

Step 4—Compute the maximum allowable depth (d_{max}) of the base using Equation 1:

$$d_{max} = f \times T_s / V_r$$

where **d_p** must be less than or equal to **d_{max}** and at least 2 feet (0.6 m) above the seasonal high groundwater table. If **d_p** does not satisfy these criteria, the surface area of the PICP must be increased or a smaller design storm must be selected. The drainage time is 48 hours.

d_{max} = 0.2 ft/hr × 48 hr/0.4 = 24 ft (288 in. or 7.31 m)   24 ft > 0.875 ft Okay

Step 5—Check the structural base thickness to be sure it has sufficient thickness to meet storage requirements plus function as a base to support 600,000 lifetime ESALs. Referring to 6% CBR column on Table 3-1 indicates a ASTM No. 57 stone base thickness of 4 in. (100 mm) and a ASTM No. 2 stone subbase of 17 in. (425 mm) or 21 in. (525 mm) total thickness. This thickness to support anticipated traffic is of course greater than the 10.5 in. thickness required to infiltrate the rainfall depth of a five-year storm falling on 1 acre of PICP receiving runoff from 2 acres of impervious asphalt. Therefore, select the thicker base/subbase solution of 21 in. (525 mm).

Step 6—Check that the bottom of the subbase is the recommended 2 ft (0.6 m) from the seasonal high water table. The total thickness of the pavement will be:
3 1/8 in. (80 mm) thick concrete pavers
2 in. (50 mm) ASTM No. 8 stone leveling course
4 in. (100 mm) ASTM No. 57 base
17 in. (425 mm) ASTM No. 2 subbase
Total thickness = 26 in. (655 mm)

Approximately 26 in. (2.2 ft or 655 mm) leaves 7.8 ft (2.4 m) to the top of the seasonal high water table. This is greater than the 2 ft (0.6 m) recommended minimum distance. A somewhat obscure consideration is the storage capacity of the layer of ASTM No. 8 crushed stone. As a factor of safety, the void space in the ASTM No. 8 layer is not part of the storage calculations. Overflow drain pipes at the perimeter of the ASTM No. 57 stone layer should be designed to remove excess water before it rises into the bedding layer and to the PICP surface.

Step 7—Check geotextile filter criteria. If geotextile is specified between the subbase and subgrade soil, it will be necessary to check the geotextile filter criteria. Sieve analysis of the soil subgrade showed that 18% passed the No. 200 (0.075 mm) sieve. Table 3-3 and 3-4 provides guidance on specifications for selecting geotextile. The designer is considering use of a geotextile that meets AASHTO M-288 Class II for average construction conditions. The product is a 6 oz/ft^2 (1.8 kg/m^2) non-woven fabric with an elongation greater than or equal to 50%, a permittivity of 1.4/sec, apparent opening size of 0.212 mm (No. 70 sieve) and grab strength of 712 N (160 lbf). This meets the AASHTO M-288 criteria in Table 3-3 and 3-4. The geotextile manufacturer specification sheet states that the fabric has a permittivity of 1.4/sec and a thickness of 1.2 mm. Therefore, estimated permeability is 1.4/sec × 1.2 mm = 1.68 mm/s = 238 in./hr. This criterion fulfills the AASHTO M-288 requirement that geotextile permeability exceed that of the soil and the standard of practice (Giroud, 1988, 1996) that the geotextile permeability is ten times that of the soil being filtered. Page 41 includes additional information and design recommendations.

Table 3-3. AASHTO M-288 Geotextile strength property requirements

Characteristic	Test Methods	Elongation < 50% per ASTM D4632		Elongation ≥ 50% per ASTM D4632	
		Class 1	Class 2	Class 1	Class 2
Grab strength	ASTM D4632	315 lb (1400 N)	247 lb (1100 N)	202 lb (900 N)	157 lb (700 N)
Sewn strength	ASTM D4632	283 lb (1260 N)	223 lb (990N)	182 lb (810 N)	142 lb (630N)
Tear strength	ASTM D4533	67 lb (300 N)	90 lb (400 N)	79 lb (350 N)	56 lb (250 N)
Puncture strength	ASTM D4833	67 lb (300 N)	90 lb (400 N)	79 lb (350 N)	56 lb (250 N)

Table 3-4. AASHTO M-288 Subsurface drainage geotextile requirements

Characteristic	Test Methods	Percent in Situ Soil Passing 0.075 mm Sieve per AASHTO T-88		
		<15	15 to 50	>50
Permittivity* (1) max. avg. roll value	ASTM D4491	0.5/sec	0.2/second	0.1/second
Apparent opening size (1) max. avg. roll value	ASTM D4751	No. 40 sieve (0.43 mm)	No. 60 sieve (0.25 mm)	No. 70 sieve (0.22 mm)
Ultraviolet stability (retained strength)	ASTM D4355	Maximum average roll value: 50% after 500 hours of exposure		

*Geotextile permeability = permittivity x geotextile thickness; e.g. 0.1/sec x 1.2 mm = 0.12 mm/sec (17 in./hr). The permeability of the geotextile should conservatively exceed an order of magnitude higher than the soil subgrade permeability.

(1)These default filtration property values are based on the predominant particles sizes of in situ soil. In addition to the default permittivity value, the engineer may require geotextile permeability and/or performance testing based on engineering design for drainage systems in problematic soil environments. Site specific geotextile design should be performed especially if one or more of the following problematic soil environments are encountered; unstable or highly erodible soils such as non-cohesive silts; gap graded soils; alternating sand/silt laminated soils; dispersive clays; and/or rock flour.

From M 288-06 (Geotextile Specifications for Highway Applications) in Standard Specifications for Transportation Materials and Methods of Sampling and Testing, 2010, by the American Assoiation of State Highway and Transportation Officials, Washington, D.C. Used by permission.

Outflow Rate and Volume Through Underdrains—If the depth of the base/subbase for the full exfiltration system is excessive, (i.e. d_p exceeds d_{max}) because, as an example, the design subgrade soil infiltration rate is not adequate to remove the water from the design storm within the designated period of time, then the design should include underdrains. The following procedure is for sizing the base / subbase for partial exfiltration designs (i.e. contains underdrains). The same symbols shown in Figure 3-2 apply, but with the following additions:

q_u = Outflow through underdrain, ft/hr.

k = Coefficient of permeability for each 6 in. (150 mm) diameter underdrain, ft/hr.

m = underdrain pipe slope, ft/ft

n = number of underdrain pipes.

T_{fill} = effective filling time of the base/subbase which is at or above the underdrain(s), hours.

T_1 = the storage time during which the water is at or above the underdrain(s), hours.

d_{below} = depth of the subbase below the underdrains, ft (m)

Equation 5 can be used to approximate the outflow rate from underdrain(s). This equation is based on Darcy's Law, which summarizes several properties that groundwater exhibits while flowing in aqui-

fers. Although the hydraulic conductivity (measure of the ease with which water can move through pore spaces of a material) of the aggregate subbase is very high (~17,000 ft/day or 5,182 m/day), the discharge rate through underdrains is limited by the cross sectional area of the pipe. As the storage volume above/around the underdrain(s) decreases, i.e., the hydraulic head or water pressure decreases; the base/subbase and in turn the underdrain(s) will drain increasingly slower. To account for this change in flow conditions within the subbase and underdrain(s) over time, a very conservative coefficient of permeability (k) of 100 ft/day (8.33 ft/hr or 2.5 m/hr) per pipe can be used to approximate the average underdrain outflow rate (VADCR 2010).

$$q_u = k \times m \qquad \text{(Equation 5)}$$

Once the outflow rate through each underdrain has been approximated, Equation 6 can be used to determine the depth of the base/subbase needed to store the design storm. To estimate the number of underdrain pipes (**n**), take the dimension of the parking lot in the direction the pipes are to be placed and divide by the desired spacing between pipes – round down to the nearest whole number.

$$d_p = \frac{\Delta Q_c R + P - fT - q_u(T_{fill})n}{V_r} \qquad \text{(Equation 6)}$$

$T_{fill} = T$ when the underdrains are at the bottom of the subbase. $T_{fill} = \frac{1}{2} T$ (approximation) when the underdrains are raised.

With full exfiltration systems, the maximum allowable drain time (d_{max}) needs to be calculated to make sure the stored water within the base/subbase does not take too long to infiltrate into the soil subgrade. However, for partial exfiltration systems, there is a second method of storage water discharge, namely the underdrains. The depth and number of underdrains are variables that can be adjusted (unlike the infiltration rate into the soil subgrade) so that the actual drain time equals or is less than the maximum allowable drain time. If the discharge of the underdrains is added to Equation 1, then:

$$d_{max} = \frac{fT_s + q_u T_1 n}{V_r} = d_p$$

Rearranging the previous creates Equation 7, with the only remaining variable (T_1) being on the left hand side.

$$T_1 = \frac{V_r d_p - fT_s}{q_u n} \qquad \text{(Equation 7)}$$

The elevation of the pipe above the soil subgrade is then calculated using Equation 8.

$$d_{below} = \frac{f(T_s - T_1)}{V_r} \qquad \text{(Equation 8)}$$

PICP can also be designed to augment detention storage needed for channel protection and/or flood control. The designer can model various approaches by factoring in storage within the base/subbase, expected infiltration and any outlet structures used as part of the design. For example, some PICP applications in the Chicago, Illinois area are designed to detain and partially infiltrate the 100-year storm for managing combined sewer overflows.

Sizing Example—Partial Exfiltration

Step 1—Assess site conditions. The site is the same one used for the previous example.

The dimensions of the 1 acre (4,047 m²) PICP area is roughly 330 feet by 1330 feet (100 meters by 405 meters). Two underdrains are proposed, with each pipe covering 165 feet (50 metres) across the shorter dimension of the PICP area. The surface slope of the PICP area is set at 1% towards an overflow bio-swale. The soil type is SC or clayey sand with a tested infiltration rate of 0.2 in./hr (1.4 x 10⁻⁶ m/sec) or a design infiltration rate of 0.1 in./hr (0.7 x 10⁻⁶ m/sec).

Step 2—Compute the increased runoff depth from the contributing area. As with the previous, all of the rainfall, being 3 in. (0.25 ft or 0.076 m), will flow from the contributing area into the PICP.

Step 3—Compute the outflow through each underdrain from Equation 5. The slope of the pipes was set at 1% (1ft /100 ft) to follow the surface slope; this not only simplifies installation but also maintains a constant cover over the pipes.

$$q_u = k \times m = 8.33 \text{ ft/hr} \times 1/100 \text{ ft/ft} = 0.0833 \text{ ft/hr}$$

Step 4—Compute the depth of the aggregate base/subbase (d_p) from Equation 6.

$$d_p = \frac{\Delta Q_c R + P - fT - q_u(T_{fill})n}{V_r} = \frac{0.25 \text{ ft (2ac./1 ac.)} + 0.25 \text{ ft} - 0.0083 \text{ ft/hr (2 hr)} - 0.0833 \text{ ft/hr(1 hr)2 pipes}}{0.4}$$

$$d_p = 1.4 \text{ ft (17 in. or 0.432 m)}$$

Step 5—Compute the storage time during which the water is at or above the underdrains (T_1) from Equation 7.

$$T_1 = \frac{V_r d_p - fT_s}{q_u n} = \frac{0.4(1.42 \text{ ft}) - 0.0083 \text{ ft/hr (48 hr)}}{0.0833 \text{ ft/hr (2 pipes)}}$$

$$T_1 = 1 \text{ hour}$$

Step 6—Compute the elevation of the underdrains (d_{below}) from Equation 8.

$$d_{below} = \frac{f(T_s - T_1)}{V_r} = \frac{0.0083 \text{ ft/hr (48 hr} - 3.1 \text{ hr)}}{0.4}$$

$$d_{below} = 0.975 \text{ ft (11.7 in. or 0.297 m)}$$

Step 7—Check the structural base thickness. On Table 3-1, a soil with a 6% CBR and 600,000 lifetime ESALs requires a ASTM No. 57 stone base thickness of 4 in. (100 mm) and a ASTM No. 2 stone sub-base of 17 in. (425 mm)—the total is 21 in. (525 mm). This thickness to support the anticipated traffic is greater than the 17 in. (432 mm) thickness required to infiltrate the design storm. Therefore, select the thicker base/subbase solution of 21 in. (525 mm).

Step 8—Check that the bottom of the subbase is the recommended 2 ft (0.6 m) from the seasonal high water table. The total thickness of the pavement will be:

3 ¹/₈ in. (80 mm) thick concrete pavers
2 in. (50 mm) ASTM No. 8 stone bedding course
4 in. (100 mm) No 57 base
17 in. (425 mm) No 2 subbase

Total thickness = 26 in. (655 mm)

Approximately 26 in. (2.17 ft or 0.66 m) minus 10 ft (3 m) leaves 7.83 ft (2.38 m) to the water table.

Step 9—Check the amount of cover over the underdrains. Confirm with the pipe supplier what the recommended cover thickness of aggregate is over the underdrain pipe; if no information is available, try to maintain at least 8 to 12 in. (200 to 300 mm).

The bottom of the pipe is 11.7 in. (0.975 ft or 0.297 m) above the bottom of the subbase. With a pipe diameter of 6 in. (150 mm), the top of the pipe is about 8.425 in. (0.7 ft or 0.214 m) below the surface. If additional aggregate cover is desired, the options are:

1. Add additional subbase material to provide the necessary cover.

2. Drop the underdrains lower down into the base. This will help increase the time required to drain the base/subbase, but will also reduce the amount of water directed away from the storm water system.

3. Recalculate with smaller diameter pipes but with a higher quantity.

The preceding is intended for sizing and preliminary design purposes only. Beyond sizing, hydrological design requires continuous simulation that models infiltration and outflow over a period of time steps as noted in Figure 3-1. This is required when using underdrains in low infiltration soils in a partial exfiltration design or a no exfiltration design. To assist in modeling water movement over time, ICPI offers a software program for PICP called *Permeable Design Pro*. It can be used to provide a more accurate solution of the peak discharge and required storage volume. It can also calculate subsurface flows via placement of drain pipes at a specified diameter, horizontal spacing, slope and distance above the soil subgrade. This enables more effective partial exfiltration designs in low infiltration clay soils. The model uses a non-proprietary drainage model called Drainage Requirements in Pavements (DRIP) developed by U.S. Federal Highway Administration (FHWA 2002).

Other Design Considerations

Soil Compaction

Soil compaction will of course decrease the infiltration rate of the soil. Infiltration reduction depends on the soil type and density. Clay soils will experience the highest reductions. However, Pitt (Pitt 2002) demonstrates that such reductions in compacted clay soils are variable and such variations allow for some infiltration. Jones (Jones 2010) also demonstrated that selected compacted clay soils in Northern California still provided a modest amount of infiltration in laboratory tests.

Soil subgrade compaction is based on designer preferences. The decrease in soil infiltration from compaction must be factored into the design infiltration rate of the soil. If the soil is not compacted in an effort to maintain higher infiltration rates, diligent use and site control of tracked construction equipment traversing excavated soil subgrade will minimize inadvertent compaction. Wheeled construction equipment should be kept from the excavated soil as these tend to concentrate loads, stress and compaction. Pedestrian applications shouldn't require deliberate soil subgrade compaction.

Many PICP installations will be over undisturbed native soils. Soil excavations typically will be 2 to 3 ft (0.6 to 0.9 m) deep and cut into consolidated soil horizons that exhibit some density and stability when wet. For vehicular applications, this subgrade layer should be evaluated by a qualified civil or geotechnical engineer for the need for compaction. If compaction is needed, then on-site infiltration tests using previously referenced ASTM methods should be conducted on test areas of compacted soil.

In some PICP projects, the soil subgrade was not compacted in order to promote infiltration. These projects were designed with fairly thick base/subbases for water storage, saw moderate traffic loads, and had adequate subgrade infiltration that reduced risks from rutting and deformation. In some cases, the PICP base is overdesigned from a structural standpoint in order to store water. Thicker bases used in PICP work in favor of not compacting the native soil subgrade.

There are other factors on sites not specifically covered in the manual that influence design decisions. The guidance of an experienced civil or geotechnical engineer familiar with local site conditions and stormwater management should be sought to confirm the suitability of the soil characteristics and possible treatments for use under PICP.

Geotextiles

Geotextiles are recommended on the sides of all PICP excavations in the absence of a full-depth concrete curb to restrain the base/subbase aggregates. Vertical placement of geotextiles helps prevent erosion of adjacent soil into the base and subbase layers. Geotextiles applied vertically against the walls of the excavation should have at least 1 ft (0.3 m) lying horizontally on the soil subgrade. The use of geotextiles placed horizontally over the entire soil subgrade is the option of the design engineer. There have been PICP applications with and without geotextiles over the soil subgrade and both conditions have performed adequately for years.

The aggregate filled joints and bedding provide a first line of filtering and trapping of sediment. This substantially reduces the amount of suspended particles entering the PICP base/subbase settling on the soil subgrade and reducing its permeability.

Geotextiles selected for use in PICP should conform to subsurface requirements in AASHTO M-288, Geotextiles for Highway Applications (AASHTO 2010). These are provided in Tables 3-3 and 3-4. Geotextile strength properties should conform to Class 1 (highest strength) if exposed to severe installation conditions with greater potential for geotextile damage. Class 2 geotextiles are typically used in PICP which often has less severe installation conditions.

Permeability and Choke Criteria for the Bedding, Base and Subbase— Ferguson (2005) provides criteria for all aggregate layers and these are noted in Table 3-5 below. D_x is the particle size at which x percent of the particles are finer. For example, D_{15} is the particle size of the aggregate for which 15% of the particles are smaller and 85% are larger. This data is obtained from the sieve analysis. The criteria are also presented as option for the user to evaluate bedding/bass/subbase layer gradations in *Permeable Design Pro* software.

Table 3-5. Filter criteria for PICP bedding, base and subbase aggregates

Permeability	D_{15} Base/D_{15} Bedding layer >5
Choke	D_{50} Base/D_{50} Bedding layer <25
	D_{15} Base/D_{85} Bedding layer <5

Permeability	D_{15} Subbase/D_{15} Base >5
Choke	D_{50} Subbase/D_{50} Base <25
	D_{15} Subbase/D_{85} Base <5

North American PICP over the past 10 years indicated that the ASTM No. 8 bedding stone chokes well into ASTM No. 57 base and this material chokes well into ASTM No. 2 subbase material. When compacted together, water easily moves through each layer to the soil subgrade. Therefore, these gradations offer high permeability while choked into each other. While one layer chokes well into the next, this characteristic should not be viewed as a contributing factor to structural stability. Salient factors that contribute to structural stability of the system under vehicular traffic include using crushed stone, hard aggregates, appropriate thicknesses, and compaction.

NRCS Curve Number Calculations

Like most structural BMPs, the hydrological and pollution abatement characteristics of PICP should be incorporated into managing runoff within the larger catchment, sub-watershed or watershed. The U.S. Department of Agriculture, Natural Resource Conservation Service (NRCS) National Engineering Handbook 630 Hydrology (USDA 2003) method is well-established and used by many agencies. The NRCS characterizes runoff from sites based on the hydrologic soil group (A – D) and land use/cover using a "curve number" or CN. The CN ranges from 0 to 100 to characterize a site or watershed with zero to 100 percent runoff.

A key variable in determining the CN for PICP is the soil infiltration capacity since infiltrated rainfall renders a lower curve number than soils with higher infiltration capacities. Therefore CNs for PICP will likely range between the 40s for A soils and in the high 70s or low 80s for C and D soils. Some caution should be exercised in applying the NRCS method to calculating runoff in catchments smaller than 5 acres (2 ha). This method is intended to calculate runoff from larger storms (2, 10, and 100 year return periods) with 24-hour durations and from larger catchments or watersheds. Therefore, the NRCS procedure tends to underestimate runoff from smaller storms in small drainage areas.

Claytor and Schueler (Claytor 1996) suggest methods to calculate runoff from small areas from smaller storms especially when water quality needs to be controlled. Schwartz (Schwartz 2010) provides guidance for applying curve numbers to pervious pavement as well as for runoff into PICP from contributing impervious areas. Ballestero (Stormcon 2010) presented methods to determine CNs based on the pre- and post-development peak flows, lag time, or from runoff depths from simple comparisons of rainfall versus runoff. The following method follows Schwartz's rationale and is the simplest assessment where:

$$Q = \frac{(P - I_a)^2}{P - I_a + S}$$

Where:
Q = Total runoff depth (in.)
P = Total precipitation depth (in.)
I_a = Initial abstraction (in.) or initial rainfall that doesn't amount to runoff
S = Storage parameter (in.) or the total stored in the PICP base/subbase reservoir that is not runoff
I = 0.05S (from Hawkins 2009)

Permeable Design Pro software calculates the CN and runoff coefficient C for user inputs on the site, specific design storms and soil infiltration rate among others. The program enables the user to conduct sensitivity analysis by changing PICP design variables that impact CN and C values.

$$Q = \frac{(P - I_a)^2}{P + 0.95S} = \frac{(P - 0.095S)^2}{P + 0.95S}$$

$$S = \frac{1000 - 10}{CN} \quad \text{or} \quad CN = \frac{1000}{S + 10}$$

The NRCS model does not account for infiltration over time. The total amount of water infiltrated over a given time (e.g. 24 hour storm) can be estimated and included in S, the storage parameter. Development, assumptions and critique of the NRCS method can be found in *Curve Number Hydrology* (Hawkins 2009).

Rational Method Calculations

The Rational Method is useful for estimating only peak runoff discharges for sizing storm sewers in watersheds up to 200 acres (80 ha). Peak discharge is found from the formula:

Q = CIA

Where:
Q = Peak discharge in ft³/second
I = Design rainfall intensity, in./hour

A = Drainage area, acres

C = Coefficient of runoff

PICP is not a storm sewer. Since the intent of the Rational Method is to find a peak or maximum flow for sewer design, the method has limited use for calculating volumes into and flowing out of PICP, and cannot be used in water quality calculations. The "C" value or coefficient of runoff in the Rational Method is a generalized value which characterizes the percentage of runoff generated from all storms. To develop a C value for all storms, PICP subbase discharge from all rainfall events would need to be estimated. This would include outflow from storms that PICP cannot store and infiltrate. Therefore, soil infiltration enters into considering a generalized PICP C value under all rainfall conditions. A reasonable PICP C value for all storms is 0.25 for PICP on high infiltration soils and 0.4 on low infiltration soils.

Applying the Rational Method to determine peak flows from PICP from a specific design storm is a simplistic and potentially inaccurate approach that doesn't incorporate PICP advantages. PICP is best designed as a detention facility as part of the conveyance or drainage system and not as land cover with a specific C value that translates to generated runoff. Besides rainfall depth, intensity, and runoff from contributing areas, PICP peak outflow design considers factors such as antecedent soil moisture, soil infiltration, soil subgrade slope, base/subbase storage, drain pipe number, size, elevation, slope, etc. If a local regulatory agency requires a PICP C value for plan approval rather than peak flows, the designer can estimate a C value by dividing outflow volume by inflow volume for a specific storm or range of storms.

Design for Water Quality Improvement

Since urbanization significantly alters the land's capacity to absorb and process water pollutants, most localities are regulating the amount of pollutants in stormwater. This is particularly the case when drinking-water supplies and fishing industries need protection. Urban stormwater pollutants and their sources are shown in Table 3-6. Total maximum daily loads or TMDLs are seeing increased use by states and cities to protect such assets. PICP is an important tool in addressing TMDLs at the site scale. The following section summarizes PICP water quality research and can assist in assigning pollutant reduction credits to PICP.

Table 3-6. Common sources of pollution in urban stormwater runoff (NVPDC 1999)

Pollutant Category Source	Solids	Nutrients	Bacteria	Dissolved oxygen demands	Metals	Oils (PAHs)* SOCs*
Soil erosion	*	*		*	*	
Cleared vegetation	*	*		*		
Fertilizers		*				
Human waste	*	*	*	*		
Animal waste	*	*	*	*		
Vehicle fuels and fluids	*			*	*	*
Fuel combustion		*			*	
Vehicle wear	*			*	*	
Industrial/houshold chemicals	*	*	*	*	*	*
Industrial processes	*	*	*	*	*	*
Paints and preservatives				*	*	*
Pesticides				*	*	

PAHs = polynuclear aromatic hydrocarbons   SOCs = synthetic organic compounds

PICP reduces pollutant concentrations and mass loads through several processes with infiltration being the primary means to reduce water volumes and pollutants.. The aggregate filters the stormwater and slows it sufficiently to allow some sedimentation to occur. Sandy soils will infiltrate more stormwater, but have less metals treatment capability. Clay soils have a high cation exchange capacity and will capture adsorb metals, but will infiltrate less. Debo and Reese (Debo 1995) recommend that for control runoff quality, the stormwater should infiltrate through at least 18 in. (0.45 m) of soil which has a minimum cation exchange capacity of 5 milliequivalents per 100 grams of dry soil.

PICP is seeing increased use in water quality volume capture because the subbase can easily store the 1 to 1.5 in. (25 to 40 mm) of water required which often accounts for 85% to 90% of all rainstorms. Many soils can infiltrate this depth within 24 to 48 hours. Additional base storage can be designed to capture 95% of all rainstorms as required for U.S. federal government facilities per Section 438 of the Energy Investment and Security Act, as well as local regulations and sustainable urban drainage design guidelines.

Studies have found that PICP encourages treatment via bacteria in the soils and beneficial bacteria growth has been found on established aggregate bases (Newman 2002). In addition, PICP can process oil drippings from vehicles (Pratt 1999).

Table 3-7 provides measured pollutant removals from a sample of studies. A summary follows on each of these studies.

Table 3-7. Monitored pollutant removals of PICP

Application	Location	Total Suspended Solids	Metals	Nutrients
Driveways (1)	Jordan Cove, CT	67%	Cu: 67% Pb: 67% Zn: 71%	TP: 34% NO3-N: 67% NH3-N: 72%
Parking lot (2)	Goldsboro, NC	71%	Zn: 88%	TP: 65% TN: 35%
Parking lot (3)	Renton, WA	--	Cu: 79% Zn: 83%	--
Parking lot (4)	King College, ON	81%	Cu: 13% Zn: 72%	TP: 53% TKN:53%

(1 – Clausen 2006) (2 – Bean 2005) (3 – Brattebo 2003) (4 – Van Seters 2007)

Clausen (Clausen 2006) monitored runoff from driveways for one year in a small residential subdivision in Waterford, Connecticut. The driveways consisted of asphalt, crushed stone and PICP over a dense-graded base. While average reduction of TSS concentrations were 67% the annual pollutant mass export in kg/ha/yr was 86% lower on the paver driveways than on the asphalt ones.

Bean (Bean 2005) listed in Table 3-5 compared runoff quantities and quality over 18 months from a small asphalt and PICP parking lot with an open-graded aggregate base at a bakery in Goldsboro, North Carolina. The study summarizes the statistical mean pollutant concentrations from 14 rainstorms and illustrates substantial pollutant reductions including 71% for TSS.

Brattebo (Brattebo 2003) investigated the effectiveness of PICP and three other permeable pavements over six years compared to asphalt in a parking lot setting near Seattle, Washington. All rainfall infiltrated the permeable pavements with almost no surface runoff. He found that the infiltrated water had, "Significantly lower levels of copper and zinc than the asphalt runoff. Motor oil was detected in 89% of samples from the asphalt runoff but not in any water sample infiltrated through the permeable pavement. Neither lead nor diesel fuel were detected in any sample. Infiltrate measured five years earlier displayed significantly higher concentrations of zinc and significantly lower concentrations of copper and lead."

Van Seters (TRCA 2007) monitored PICP infiltrate into the soil subgrades and asphalt runoff over three years from a heavily used parking lot. He also compared pollutants in soils under and next to six PICP sites 3 to 16 years old in Ontario. There were no increases in oils (PAHs), iron, lead, zinc, copper in soils under the PICPs compared to soils adjacent to them. Chlorides saw some increase under the PICP sites and would be expected under all permeable pavements subject to snow and deicers. Van Seters also documented the condition of the six PICP sites and found that they were providing adequate structural support after years of use.

Other studies demonstrate the ability of PICP to reduce pollutants. James (James 1997) examined surface runoff from nine rainstorms over four months from asphalt, concrete pavers and PICP. He also measured pollutants in the PICP base and subbase. The PICP rendered a 97% reduction of total suspended solids compared to surface runoff generated by the asphalt surface. Similar differences were indicated by solids sampled in water leaving the PICP subbase.

Collins (2007) researched a municipal parking lot in Kinston, North Carolina consisting of pervious concrete (PC), two types of PICP and concrete grid pavement filled with sand, and asphalt. The site was located in poorly drained soils, and all permeable sections were underlain by an open-graded aggregate base with perforated pipe underdrains. All sections were monitored from June 2006 to July 2007 for hydrologic and water quality. Not surprisingly, all permeable pavements substantially reduced surface runoff volumes and peak flow rates when compared to standard asphalt. The grids demonstrated better nutrient removal due to the sand in the openings. The conclusions noted that various permeable pavement types be treated similarly with respect to runoff reduction (assuming similar base/subbases). The report recommended further research on nitrogen or phosphorous removal so that these can earn credits in North Carolina stormwater regulations.

PICP nutrient reduction capabilities can be enhanced by detaining water in the subbase for over 24 hours for de-nitrification as noted earlier. Any infiltration will of course reduce the water volumes and mass outflow of nutrients and should be accounted for in pollutant credit programs from provincial/ state and local agencies. Specially coated aggregates in the joints as well as the base can also reduce nutrients.

Some agencies encourage the use of sand filters under PICP as a means to reduce nutrients. Their effectiveness, initial and maintenance costs should be weighed against other design options for nutrient reductions. Sand filters will incur additional construction expense and this can be reduced by placing sand filters under the subbase at the down slope end of a PICP area. The disadvantage of sand filters is that they will eventually require removal and restoration. Therefore concentrating their location in the down slope areas of the site can help reduce future maintenance costs and site disruptions. Simply storing water for and slowly releasing it over 48 hours can be less expensive alternative as long as there is a carbon source in the base/subbase. A second approach useful for nutrient reduction can occur on sloping sites by creating intermittent berms in the soil subgrade. These enable settlement of suspended solids and encourage de-nitrification.

A third alternative is directing using a "treatment train" approach where PICP initially filters runoff and remaining water is directed to bioswales or rain gardens adjacent to the PICP for additional processing and nutrient reduction. There may be additional BMPs used to remove nutrients as the water moves through the watershed. Finally, another technique for nutrient reduction is using jointing and bedding aggregates coated with chemicals. The coated aggregates have an effective life of seven to ten years.

Since PICP reduces volumes in many applications, agencies should include pollutant reduction concomitant with volume reduction credits. One example of the impact of PICP on volume and pollutant reductions is a study by the City of Ann Arbor, Michigan. The project retrofitted the outer edges of an existing asphalt street with PICP. In the summary of his report, Dierks (Dierks 2009) characterizes the project as follows: "The monitoring included pre- and post-construction flow and water quality data col-

lected approximately three years apart at the same locations.... Event mean concentrations (EMCs) for total suspended solids, total phosphorus (TP), orthophosphate (OP), total copper and total zinc were reduced between 20% and 90% for all constituents. Except for TP and OP, total load reductions are attributable to event volume reductions. For TP and OP, load reductions are a function of both EMC and event volume reductions."

Some state BMP manuals include volume reduction in recognizing pollutant credits for PICP. Table 3-8 summarizes these credits for four states.

Table 3-8. Permeable pavement pollutant credits from various states (MIDS 2011)

Design	Volume Reduction	Total Phosphorous EMC Reduction				Total Suspended Solids EMC Reduction		
	VA	VA	NH	PA	MN	VA	NH	PA
No underdrains	75%	25%	65%		80%	75%	90%	
With underdrains	45%	25%	45%	85%	80%	75%	90%	85%

EMC = Event mean concentration

VA = Virginia; NH = New Hampshire; PA = Pennsylvania; MN = Minnesota

Note: The Virginia Department of Conservation and Recreation offers 25% total nitrogen removal credit on an EMC (event mean concentration) basis. In addition, credits are given for mass load removal of total phosphorous and total nitrogen. These are 59% and 81% for no underdrain and underdrain designs, respectively.

Finally, of the many BMPs used to reduce pollutants, gravel filters (i.e., PICP base/subbases) have been show to be effective and even in winter months. Roseen (Roseen 2009) evaluated the winter performance in New Hampshire of various LID practices using gravel filters including those in porous asphalt and found that all "have a high level of functionality during winter months and that frozen filter media do not reduce performance." Since PICP uses gravel filter media, winter performance in reducing runoff pollutants can be expected.

Section 4. Construction

Construction Overview

PICP construction for parking lots and roads involves the steps listed below. This Section provides details on them and explains some variations depending on the application. The end of this Section includes a guide construction specification. The guide specification is available on www.icpi.org and can be downloaded and edited to project conditions.

- Attend the pre-construction meeting
- Plan site access and keep PICP materials free from sediment
- Excavate soil or an existing pavement
- Avoid soil compaction unless required in the plans and specifications
- Install geotextiles, impermeable liners and drain pipes if required in the plans and specifications
- Place and compact the aggregate subbase
- Install curbs or other edge restraints
- Place and compact the aggregate base
- Place and screed the bedding layer
- Install pavers manually or with mechanical installation equipment
- Fill the paver joints and sweep the surface clean
- Compact the pavers
- Top up joints with joint filling stone as needed and sweep the surface clean

Figure 4-1. Special attention to many details makes PICP construction successful. This mechanically installed project is one of the largest PICP parking lots—about 7.5 acres (3 ha)—at a car dealership in Vancouver, Washington.

Attend the pre-construction meeting—For commercial and municipal projects, the specifications should include a pre-construction meeting. The pre-construction meeting is held to discuss methods of accomplishing all phases of the construction operation, contingency planning, and standards of workmanship. The general contractor typically provides the meeting facility, meeting date and time. Representatives from the following entities should be present;

1. Contractor superintendent.
2. PICP subcontractor foreman.
3. Concrete paving unit manufacturer's representative.
4. Testing laboratory (ies) representative(s).
5. Engineer or representative.

The following items should be discussed and determined:

1. Test panel (mock-up) location and dimensions.
2. Methods for keeping all materials free from sediment during storage, placement, and on completed areas.

3. Methods for checking slopes, surface tolerances, and elevations.
4. Concrete paving unit delivery method(s), timing, storage location(s) on the site, staging, paving start point(s) and direction(s).
5. Anticipated daily paving production and actual record.
6. Diagrams of paving laying/layer pattern and joining layers as indicated on the drawings
7. Monitoring/verifying paver dimensional tolerances in the manufacturing facility and on-site if the concrete paving units are mechanically installed.
8. Testing intervals for sieve analyses of aggregates and for the concrete paving units.
9. Method(s) for tagging and numbering concrete unit paving packages delivered to the site.
10. Testing lab location, test methods, report delivery, contents and timing.
11. Engineer inspection intervals and procedures for correcting work that does not conform to the project specifications.

Plan site access and keeping PICP materials free from sediment—Preventing and diverting sediment from entering the aggregates and pavement surface during construction **must be the highest priority**. Extra care must be applied to keeping sediment completely away from aggregates stored on site as well as the PICP. In some cases, it may be necessary to construct PICP before other soil-disturbing construction is completed. The options below are for ensuring that the PICP does not become contaminated with sediment from construction vehicles. The options below are in ascending cost order. One or more of these options should be decided in the project planning stages and included in the specifications and drawings.

(1) Construct the aggregate subbase and base and protect the surface of the base aggregate with geotextile and an additional 2 in. (50 mm) thick layer of the same base aggregate over the geotextile. Thicken this layer at transitions to match elevations of adjacent pavement surfaces subject to vehicular traffic. A similar more costly approach can be taken using a temporary asphalt wearing course rather than the additional base aggregate and geotextile. When construction traffic has ceased and adjacent soils are vegetated or stabilized with erosion control mats, remove geotextile and soiled aggregate (or the asphalt) and install the remainder of the PICP system per the project specifications.

(2) Install the PICP first and allow construction traffic to use the finished PICP surface. When construction traffic has ceased and adjacent soils are stabilized with vegetation or erosion control mats, clean the PICP surface and joints with a vacuum machine capable of removing an inch (25 mm) of the stone from the joints. Vacuum a test area and inspect the joints when stone is removed to be sure there are no visible traces of sediment on the stone remaining in the joints. If it is visible, then vacuum out jointing stones until no sediment is present. Fill the joints with clean stones and sweep the PICP surface clean.

(3) Protect finished PICP system by covering the surface with a woven geotextile and a minimum 2 in. thick ASTM No. 8 open-graded aggregate layer. This aggregate layer and geotextile are removed upon project completion and when adjacent soils are stabilized with vegetation or erosion control mats. The PICP surface is swept clean.

(4) Establish temporary road or roads for site access that do not allow construction vehicle traffic to ride over and contaminate the PICP base materials and/or surface with mud and sediment. Other trades on the jobsite need to be informed on using temporary road(s) and staying off the PICP. The temporary road is removed upon completion of construction and opening of the PICP surface to traffic.

Other practices such as keeping muddy construction equipment away from the PICP, installing silt fences, staged excavation, and temporary drainage swales that divert runoff away from the area will make the difference between a pavement that infiltrates well or poorly. A simple technology that may be more effective than silt fences can help block sediment from eroding from bare soil. This consists of

plastic temporary curbs with fabric in them to block the movement sediment from bare soil. Figure 4-2 illustrates this device.

Another more involved practice is a washing station for truck tires. Larger PICP projects may require this level of cleanliness as trucks enter a muddy PICP site. Figure 4-3 illustrates truck washing equipment which naturally requires disposal of dewatered sediment.

Excavate soil or an existing pavement—In some cases, the excavated area for base and PICP can be used as a sediment trap if there is time between the excavation and aggregate base installation. This is done by excavating within 6 in. (150 mm) of the final bottom elevation. This area can contain water during storms over the construction period and exit via temporary drain pipes. Heavy equipment should be kept from this area to prevent compaction. If equipment needs to traverse the bottom of the excavation, tracked vehicles can reduce the risk of soil compaction. As the project progresses, sediment and the remaining soil depth can be excavated to the final grade immediately before installing the aggregate subbase and base. Depending on the project design, this technique might eliminate the need for a separate sediment basin during construction.

Avoid soil compaction unless required in the plans and specifications—As discussed previously, soil compaction as part of the design is the engineer's decision and should be executed according the project specifications. If compaction is not specified, the initial undisturbed soil infiltration should be carefully maintained during excavation and construction as this will enable the base to drain as designed. If the soil is inadvertently compacted by equipment during construction, there will be substantial loss of infiltration. A loss may be acceptable if the infiltration rate of the soil when compacted was initially considered during design and in drainage calculations.

Compacted soil can be remedied by scarifying to increase its infiltration. This is done by back-dragging loader bucket teeth across the soil prior to placing the aggregate subbase. An interesting experiment by Tyner (2009) demonstrated substantial increase in soil infiltration rates after various treatments with construction equipment on clay soils. He compared infiltration rates on an untreated area to soil trenched and backfilled with stone aggregate; soil ripped with a subsoiler; and placement of shallow boreholes backfilled with sand. The average exfiltration rates were 0.3 in. (0.8 cm) per day (control), 1.8 in. (4.6 cm) per day (borehole), 3.8 in. (10.0 cm) per day (ripped), and 10.8 in. (25.8 cm) per day (trenched).

Figure 4-2. This temporary permeable edging around bare soil replaces silt fencing because it restrains sediment while allowing water to pass.

Figure 4-3. Larger PICP projects may require tire washing equipment for trucks to keep mud from contaminating PICP aggregates.

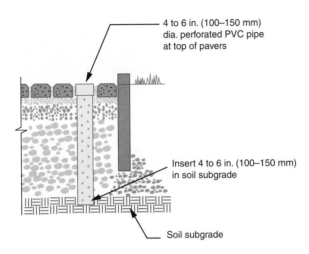

4 to 6 in. (100–150 mm) dia. perforated PVC pipe at top of pavers

Insert 4 to 6 in. (100–150 mm) in soil subgrade

Soil subgrade

Figure 4-4. Observation well into PICP base and subbase with top accessible directly from the surface to observe drain down rate.

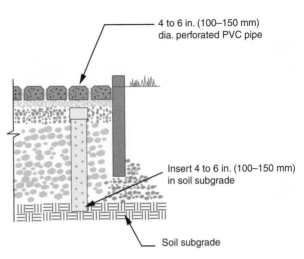

4 to 6 in. (100–150 mm) dia. perforated PVC pipe

Insert 4 to 6 in. (100–150 mm) in soil subgrade

Soil subgrade

Figure 4-5. Observation well with top hidden under pavers and bedding to obscure from vandals.

Install geotextiles, impermeable liners and drain pipes if required in the plans and specifications—Geotextiles are used in some permeable pavement applications per the design engineer. If there are no concrete curbs and soil is restraining the sides of the base/subbase at its perimeter, then geotextile should be applied to prevent erosion of soil into the base/subbase aggregates. Geotextile is applied vertically against the soil with at least 1 ft (0.3 m) extending horizontally under the subbase and resting on the soil subgrade. Geotextile specifications were covered in Section 3. A minimum 1 ft (0.3 m) overlap is recommended in well-drained soils and 2 ft (0.6 m) overlap on poor-draining weaker soils (CBR<5%).

When specified, impermeable liners require assembly per manufacturer's instructions at the job site. Once assembled, they should be tested for leaks with special attention to seams and pipe penetrations.

Drain pipes are installed according to plans and specifications. Designs should have curb cut-outs or drain pipes from the PICP entering swales or storm sewer catch basins to handle overflow conditions. Plastic pipes in bases subject to traffic should withstand repeated vehicular loads. A minimum of 12 in. (300 mm) aggregate cover is recommended over drainpipes to protect them from damage during subbase or base compaction.

If there is a risk of drain pipe damage, consider using a heavy gauge pipe or test the pipe and base in a trial area with compaction equipment prior to placing and compacting a large area. Perforations in pipes should terminate 1 ft (0.3 m) short of the sides of the opening for the base. When corrugated metal drain pipes are used, they should be aluminized, and aluminized pipe in contact with concrete should be coated to prevent corrosion. Perforated drain pipes should have caps fastened to the upslope ends. Daylighted drain pipes require wire mesh over the openings to keep out debris and animals.

Observation Wells —A 4 to 6 in. (100 to 150 mm) diameter vertical perforated pipe that serves as an observation well is recommended in PICP subject to vehicular traffic. The pipe

Figure 4-6. A 10 ton (9 T) vibratory roller compactor settles ASTM No. 2 stone subbase for a large shopping center parking lot.

Permeable Interlocking Concrete Pavements

Figure 4-7. A 10 ton (9 T) roller compacts the ASTM No. 57 base.

Figure 4-8. A 13,500 (60 kN) vibratory plate compactor is used on this ASTM No. 57 stone base.

should be kept vertical during filling of the excavated area with open-graded aggregate and during compaction. The bottom of the pipe can be forced into the soil subgrade and held in place during base/subbase filling and compaction. The pipe should be located in the lowest elevation and a minimum of 3 ft (1 m) from the PICP side. Figures 4-4 and 4-5 illustrate a well accessible from the surface and another with the pipe under the pavers to prevent damage from vandals.

Place and compact the aggregate subbase—ASTM No. 2 subbase material should be spread in minimum 6 in. (150 mm) lifts. Compaction is typically done with a 10 t (9 T) steel vibratory roller or a 13,500 lbf (60 kN) plate compactor. Greater lift thicknesses are normal (i.e., 12 in. or a 0.3 m) when using either of these compactors. When using a roller, the first two passes are in vibratory mode and the last two are in static mode. Compaction is completed when no visible movement can be seen in the base when rolled by the compactor. Plate compactors with compaction indicators should be used to determine when compaction is completed. Stones will compact more completely if moistened during compaction. Aggregates should not be crushed by the compactor. Figure 4-6 illustrates a vibratory roller compacted ASTM No. 2 stone subbase.

Place and compact the aggregate base—The ASTM No. 57 base layer is spread and compacted as one 4 in. (100 mm) lift. Again, stone materials should be moist during compaction for better consolidation. Like the subbase aggregate, the initial passes with the roller can be with vibration to consolidate the base material as shown in Figure 4-7. The final passes should be without vibration. A 13,500 lbf (60 kN) plate compactor (Figure 4-8) also can be used to compact the ASTM No. 57 base layer.

Equipment drivers should avoid rapid acceleration, hard braking, or sharp turning when driving on the compacted ASTM No. 2 subbase and on the ASTM No. 57 base. Tracked equipment is recommended. If the subbase or base surfaces are disturbed, they should be re-leveled and re-compacted.

A test section of the subbase and base should be constructed initially for compaction monitoring. The section will indicate settlement of the pavement section, and be used to monitor and prevent crushing of the aggregate. The area should be used to train in experienced construction personnel on compaction techniques.

Some designers prefer field measurement of subbase and base densities after compaction. If nuclear density gauge testing is desired, it cannot effectively be done on the ASTM No. 2 subbase. However, density testing can be done in backscatter mode on the ASTM No. 57 base layer (Figure 4-9). The guide construction specification in this Section includes a compaction testing method for the ASTM No. 57 base

Figure 4-9. Density testing with a nuclear gauge in backscatter mode can help assess consistent density of the ASTM No. 57 base layer.

Figure 4-10. A base stiffness gauge can also be used to assess compacted density of aggregates.

layer. The purpose of this test method is to attain consistent density. Besides nuclear density gauges, (non-nuclear) stiffness gauges may also be used to assess compacted base density (Figure 4-10).

Stabilized Bases—While not common, open-graded bases can be stabilized with asphalt or cement, placed, and compacted. Stabilized bases (and subbases) can increase the structural design life of PICP. Asphalt or cement coating the open-graded aggregate will likely reduce a modest amount of its water storage capacity. However, stabilization can increase its structural capacity to extend pavement life or be used in area subject to concentrated wheel loads. Pervious concrete also can provide a base and/or subbase option over weak, slow draining soils. The ASTM No. 8 bedding layer is generally not stabilized. A pavement engineer experienced in stabilized base design and practice should be consulted for PICP designs with stabilized bases.

Place and screed the bedding layer—When subbase and base lifts are compacted the surface should then be topped with a 2 in. (50 mm) thick layer of moist ASTM No. 8 crushed stone bedding layer. This layer is screeded and leveled over the ASTM No. 57 base. Metal rails are placed on the compacted ASTM No. 57 layer and are used to guide screeding elevations. Various sizes of screeding equipment can be used ranging from hand tools, bucket screeds powered manually or by machine, or a modified asphalt spread that uses a laser guidance system to maintain elevations. Figures 4-11 through 4-14 illustrate examples of screeding equipment. A moist bedding layer will facilitate screeding.

The surface tolerance of the screeded ASTM No. 8 bedding material should be ±3/8 in. over 10 ft. (±10 mm over 3 m). The concrete pavers should be placed immediately after the ASTM No. 8 stone bedding is placed and screeded. Construction equipment and foot traffic should be kept off the screeded layer.

Install curbs or other edge restraints—The selection of edge restraints depends on whether the PICP is for pedestrian, residential driveway or vehicular use. Table 4-1 summarizes recommended by edge restraint type based on the application.

Figure 4-11. A hand screed is used for screeding the bedding layer in small areas.

Figure 4-12. A bucket screed powered manually is used to screed parking spaces.

Figure 4-13. For larger areas, bucket screeds can be pulled with equipment to accelerate the screeding process.

Figure 4-14. An asphalt type spreader specifically designed for spreading bedding stone uses a laser guidance system to keep elevations consistent while spreading.

Table 4-1. Recommended edge restraints for PICP

Edge Restraint Type	Pedestrian Only	Residential Driveway	Parking lot or street
Cast-in-place concrete curb	Yes	Yes	Yes
Precast concrete curb	Yes	Yes	Yes
Cut stone curb	Yes	Yes	Yes
Compacted, dense-graded berms around PICP base perimeter with spiked metal or plastic edging to restrain Pavers	Yes	Yes	No
Troweled concrete toe	Yes	No	No

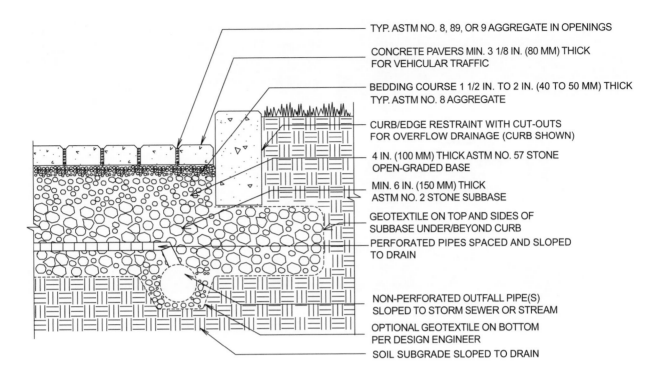

TYP. ASTM NO. 8, 89, OR 9 AGGREGATE IN OPENINGS

CONCRETE PAVERS MIN. 3 1/8 IN. (80 MM) THICK
FOR VEHICULAR TRAFFIC

BEDDING COURSE 1 1/2 IN. TO 2 IN. (40 TO 50 MM) THICK
TYP. ASTM NO. 8 AGGREGATE

CURB/EDGE RESTRAINT WITH CUT-OUTS
FOR OVERFLOW DRAINAGE (CURB SHOWN)

4 IN. (100 MM) THICK ASTM NO. 57 STONE
OPEN-GRADED BASE

MIN. 6 IN. (150 MM) THICK
ASTM NO. 2 STONE SUBBASE

GEOTEXTILE ON TOP AND SIDES OF
SUBBASE UNDER/BEYOND CURB

PERFORATED PIPES SPACED AND SLOPED
TO DRAIN

NON-PERFORATED OUTFALL PIPE(S)
SLOPED TO STORM SEWER OR STREAM

OPTIONAL GEOTEXTILE ON BOTTOM
PER DESIGN ENGINEER

SOIL SUBGRADE SLOPED TO DRAIN

Figure 4-15. Typical cast-in-place concrete curb sits on the ASTM No. 2 stone subbase. Note that the ASTM No. 2 stone requires geotextile along its sides to prevent migration of soil into it.

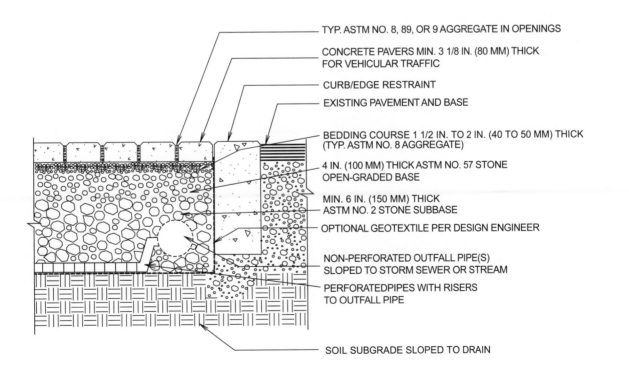

TYP. ASTM NO. 8, 89, OR 9 AGGREGATE IN OPENINGS

CONCRETE PAVERS MIN. 3 1/8 IN. (80 MM) THICK
FOR VEHICULAR TRAFFIC

CURB/EDGE RESTRAINT

EXISTING PAVEMENT AND BASE

BEDDING COURSE 1 1/2 IN. TO 2 IN. (40 TO 50 MM) THICK
(TYP. ASTM NO. 8 AGGREGATE)

4 IN. (100 MM) THICK ASTM NO. 57 STONE
OPEN-GRADED BASE

MIN. 6 IN. (150 MM) THICK
ASTM NO. 2 STONE SUBBASE

OPTIONAL GEOTEXTILE PER DESIGN ENGINEER

NON-PERFORATED OUTFALL PIPE(S)
SLOPED TO STORM SEWER OR STREAM

PERFORATEDPIPES WITH RISERS
TO OUTFALL PIPE

SOIL SUBGRADE SLOPED TO DRAIN

Figure 4-16. Typical cast-in-place concrete curb divides PICP from an adjacent impervious pavement.

Cast-in-place concrete, precast concrete and cut stone curbs are typically a minimum of 9 in. (225 mm) high and rest on the compacted ASTM No. 2 stone subbase. Consideration should be given to installing a concrete haunch under precast concrete or stone curbs. Curbs may be higher than 9 in, (225 mm) if they hold back grass, a sidewalk, bioswale or other structure. Figure 4-15 illustrate typical curb cross section.

If PICP is adjacent to existing impervious asphalt or concrete pavement, curbs level with the permeable and impervious surfaces are used. The curb should extend the full depth of the base under the impermeable pavement to protect its base from becoming weakened from excessive water. Another option is to separate the two bases with an impermeable liner. Figure 4-16 shows a full-depth concrete curb between impervious pavement and PICP.

The risk of water weakening the base under the impervious pavement can be substantially decreased by sloping the soil subgrade under the PICP away from the impervious pavement base and by using perforated drain pipes to remove water before it can collect next to the base supporting the impervious pavement. Curbs installed against existing impervious pavement and base may cause erosion and weakening of the base from excavation due to installing the PICP. Eroded spaces can be filled with concrete to support the asphalt or concrete surface and base next to the curb.

For pedestrian areas and residential driveways, an edge restraint option is using compacted, dense-graded berms around PICP base perimeter with plastic or metal edging fastened to their surface. The dense-graded base is a foundation for metal or plastic edging secured with steel spikes. These edge

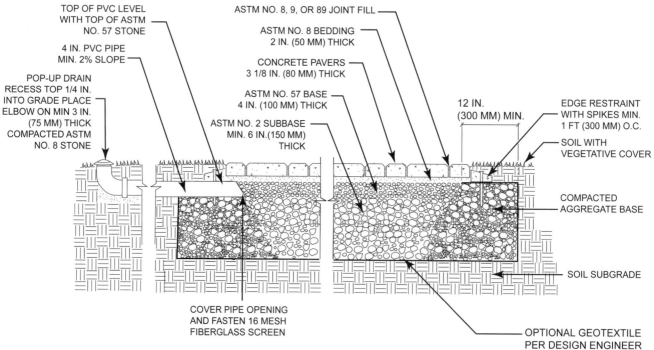

NOTES:
1. DESIGN, MATERIAL AND CONSTRUCTION GUIDELINES TO FOLLOW ICPI GUIDE SPECIFICATIONS.
2. DAYLIGHT DRAIN PIPE TO DRAINAGE SWALE, USE POP-UP DRAIN IN YARD (AS SHOWN) OR CONNECT TO STORM SEWER.
3. APPLY WATERPROOF MEMBRANE VERTICALLY AGAINST HOUSE FOUNDATION PRIOR TO PLACING SUBBASE AND BASE.
4. ALL SOIL SUBGRADES SHALL SLOPE TOWARD STREET.
5. SUBGRADE SOIL MAXIMUM CROSS SLOPE IS 0.5%. MAXIMUM LONGITUDINAL SLOPE IS 2% TOWARD STREET.
6. USE SOIL BERMS FOR LONGITUDINAL SOIL SUBGRADE SLOPES EXCEEDING 2% TOWARD STREET.
7. 5% MAXIMUM SURFACE SLOPE.
8. THICKER SUBBASSE AND/OR ADDITIONAL DRAIN PIPES MAY BE REQUIRED IF DRIVEWAY RECEIVES RUNOFF FROM ADJACENT IMPERVIOUS SURFACES OR ROOFS.

Figure 4-17. Typical cross section detail using a dense-graded base berm as a foundation for anchoring metal or plastic edge restraints.

Figure 4-18. Perimeter berms made with dense-graded base are in place prior to placing open-graded aggregate in the driveway.

Figure 4-19. Compacting the berms along the perimeter and the PICP base

Figure 4-20. Plastic edge restraint is spiked into the dense-graded base berms so it can hold the pavers in place during compaction and service.

Figure 4-21. A PICP walk with a troweled concrete toe sits next to a driveway with a formed and cast-in-place concrete curb. Concrete toes should only be used for pedestrian applications.

restraints are installed on the dense-graded berms in a manner identical to those on interlocking concrete pavement driveways. Figure 4-17 shows a typical cross section of this construction and Figure 4-18 illustrates the berms in place prior to filling the driveway with open-graded aggregate. Figure 4-19 shows compaction of both types of bases. Edge restraints and then spiked into the dense-graded base berms, bedding material screeded and pavers installed. Figure 4-20 shows the pavers in place against a plastic edge restraint spiked or nailed into the dense-graded base. The edge restraint contains some of the bedding layer such that at least the bottom 1/2 in. (13 mm) of the pavers is also contained by the edging.

Figure 4-21 illustrates a concrete toe placed against a sidewalk behind a driveway with a cast-in-place concrete edge. Concrete toes rest on the base extending at least 6 in. (150 mm) past the paver edges. The concrete should be a minimum of 4 in. (100 mm) wide by 3 in. (75 mm) deep so that it can re-

Figure 4-22 and 4-23. Mechanical equipment accelerated installation of a parking lot in Illinois and a street in Oregon.

strain the pavers. Concrete mixed on the job site should use an approximate 5:1 aggregate to cement content. Once prepared in a concrete mixer, the concrete toe is typically spread with a shovel and smoothed with trowel. Pavers are compacted once the concrete has hardened. This type of edging is not recommended in cold climate regions because of the high risk of cracking.

Install the pavers manually or with mechanical installation equipment—After screeding the bedding material, the pavers are placed on this layer. Paver installation can be by hand or with mechanical equipment. Mechanized installation may be a cost efficient means to install the units and will reduce installation time. Figure 4-22 and 4-23 shows mechanized equipment placing permeable paver layers manufactured for placement in their final laying pattern. Mechanical installation requires careful planning including selection available paver layer patterns from local manufacturers and well-orchestrated material flow logistics in order to gain efficiencies. For further information on mechanical installation, consult *ICPI Tech Spec 11—Mechanical Installation of Interlocking Concrete Pavements* and *ICPI Tech Spec 15—A Guide for the Construction of Mechanically Installed Interlocking Concrete Pavements.*

An important consideration with mechanical installation projects on projects over 50,000 sf (5,000 m²) is monitoring paver production mold wear so that paver layers can quickly fit next to each other when installed. Among many topics, *Tech Spec 15* covers managing dimensional growth of pavers and provides means for confirming dimensions of the pavers at the factory and on the job site. Managing paver dimensions should be decided between the paver manufacturer and paver installation contractor and confirmed at the pre-construction meeting.

Border courses consisting of mostly whole (uncut) pavers are typically used against curbs at PICP edges and at transitions to other pavement surfaces. Paving units abutting border courses should be cut to fill spaces prior to compaction. Cut units should be no smaller than one-third of a whole unit if subject to tires. All installed units should have joints filled and compacted within 6 ft (2 m) of the laying face at the end of each day.

Filling the paver joints and sweep the surface clean—The paver joints are filled with ASTM No. 8, 89 or 9 stone. Depending on the PICP area, spreading and sweeping can be done with shovels and brooms, or larger areas with Bobcats and swept into the paver joints with powered brooms or sweep-

ers. Once the joints are full (within 1/4 in. or 6 mm of the paver surface), the surface must be swept clean prior to compaction as loose stones on the surface can mar the pavers when in contact with a plate compactor. Figure 4-24 illustrate various filling and sweeping methods.

Compact the pavers—After the PICP surface is swept clean, it is compacted with a plate compactor. A minimum of two passes should be made with the second pass in a perpendicular direction from the first pass. The path of the plate compactor should overlap several inches (cm). For paving units 3 1/8 to 4 in. (80 to 100 mm) thick, the plate compactor should exert a minimum 5,000 lbf (22 kN) at 75 to 90 Hz. Figure 4-25 shows permeable pavers being compacted for a street project using a large plate compactor.

Top up joints with joint filling stone as needed and sweep the surface clean—Compaction can cause some settlement of the stones inside the joints. If the stones are more than 1/4 in. (6 mm) from the paver surface, they should be topped up to this level with additional stones. The paver surface should be swept clean prior to opening the PICP to traffic.

Aggregates in the paver joints can settle in early in the life of the pavement. Some settlement can be reduced through consistent, thorough compaction of the base, pavers and bedding layers. However, it is advisable for the contractor to return to the site after six months, inspect the joints and top them up with aggregate if they have settled to more than 1/4 in. (6 mm) below the paver surface. This service should be included in the construction specifications.

Construction Checklist

The following provides a convenient checklist for contractors and project inspectors.

Pre-construction meeting

- ❏ Walk through site with builder/contractor/subcontractor to review erosion and sediment control plan/stormwater pollution prevention plan or SWPPP)
- ❏ Determine when PICP is built in project construction sequence; before or after building construction, and measures for PICP protection and surface cleaning
- ❏ Aggregate material locations identified (hard surface or on geotextile)
- ❏ Sediment management
    - ❏ Access routes for delivery and construction vehicles identified
    - ❏ Vehicle tire/track washing station (if specified in E&S plan/SWPPP) location/ maintenance

Figure 4-24. Various methods of filling and sweeping PICP joints.

Figure 4-25. PICP paver compaction shows that pavers need to be set about 1 in. (25 mm) above their final elevation (after compaction) to account for downward movement.

Excavation

☐ Utilities located and marked by local service
☐ Excavated area marked with paint and/or stakes
☐ Excavation size and location conforms to plan
☐ Sediment management
　☐ Excavation hole as sediment trap: cleaned immediately before subbase stone placement and runoff sources with sediment diverted away from the PICP, or
　☐ All runoff diverted away from excavated area.

　☐ Temporary soil stockpiles should be protected from run-on, run-off from adjacent areas and from erosion by wind.
　☐ Ensure linear sediment barriers (if used) are properly installed, free of accumulated litter, and built up sediment less than 1/3 the height of the barrier.
　☐ No runoff enters PICP until soils stabilized in area draining to PICP
☐ Foundation walls:
　☐ At least 10 ft (3 m) from foundation walls with no waterproofing or drainage
☐ At least 100 ft (30 m) from municipal water supply wells
☐ Soil subgrade: rocks and roots removed, voids refilled with permeable soil
☐ Soil compacted to specifications (if required) and field tested with density measurements per specifications
☐ No groundwater seepage or standing water. If so dewatering or dewatering permit may be required.

Geotextile (if specified)

☐ Meets specifications
☐ Placement and down slope overlap (min. 2 ft or 0.6 m) conform to specifications and drawings
☐ Sides of excavation covered with geotextile prior to placing aggregate base/subbase
☐ No tears or holes
☐ No wrinkles, pulled taught and staked

Impermeable Liner (if specified)

❏ Meets specifications
❏ Placement, field welding, and seals at pipe penetrations done per specifications

Drain pipes/observations wells

❏ Size, perforations, locations, slope, and outfalls meet specifications and drawings
❏ Verify elevation of overflow pipes

Subbase, base, bedding and jointing aggregates

❏ Sieve analysis from quarry conforms to specifications
❏ Spread (not dumped) with a front-end loader to avoid aggregate segregation
❏ Storage on hard surface or geotextile to keep sediment-free
❏ Thickness, placement, compaction and surface tolerances meet specifications and drawings

Edge restraints

❏ Elevation, placement, and materials meet specifications and drawings

Permeable interlocking concrete pavers

❏ Meet ASTM/CSA standards (as applicable) per manufacturer's test results
❏ Elevations, slope, laying pattern, joint widths, and placement/compaction meet drawings and specifications
❏ No cut paver subject to tire traffic is less than 1/3 of a whole paver
❏ All pavers within 6 ft (2 m) of the laying face fully compacted at the completion of each day
❏ Surface tolerance of compacted pavers deviate no more than ±3/8 (±10 mm) under a 10 ft (3 m) long straightedge

Final inspection

❏ Surface swept clean
❏ Elevations and slope(s) conform to drawings
❏ Transitions to impervious paved areas separated with edge restraints
❏ Surface elevation of pavers 1/8 to 3/8 in. (3 to 10 mm) above adjacent drainage inlets, concrete collars or channels (for non-ADA accessible paths of travel); to ¼ in. or 6 mm (for ADA accessible paths of travel)
❏ Lippage: no greater than 1/8 in. (3 mm) difference in height between adjacent pavers
❏ Bond lines for paver courses: ±1/2 in. (±15 mm) over a 50 ft (15 m) string line
❏ Stabilization of soil in area draining into permeable pavement (min. 20 ft (6 m) wide vegetative strips recommended)
❏ Drainage swales or storm sewer inlets for emergency overflow. If storm sewer inlets are used, confirm overflow drainage to them.
❏ Runoff from non-vegetated soil diverted from PICP surface
❏ Test surface for infiltration rate per specifications using ASTM C1701; minimum 100 in./hr (2500 mm/hr) recommended

PICP Specialist Course

ICPI offers a 1 1/2 day PICP Specialist Course for those interested in training on PICP best construction practices. This course is referenced as a requirement in an increasing number of commercial, municipal and state specifications. The classroom program is for contractors who are presently doing residential

and/or commercial interlocking concrete pavement installations, and who wish to move into the permeable pavement market. Participants should be experienced contractors, and it is recommended (but not required) that participants have completed the ICPI Concrete Paver Installer Course. This course is approved for ICPI installer continuing education and ICPI Certified Installers earn 11 continuing education credits.

The course cover PICP systems, job planning and documentation, job layout, flow and estimating quantities, soil & site characteristics, subbase and base materials, edge restraints, bedding and jointing materials, paver selection and installation, and maintenance. Participants who take the course receive a student manual. Participants that earn a passing grade on the exam will receive a Record of Completion for the course. The Record of Completion does not expire, and will not require a renewal. Other courses include Concrete Paver Installer certification and Commercial Paver Technician. If these are taken, then they can earn a PICP Specialist designation upon taking the PICP course. Most classes are sponsored by local ICPI manufacturing members. Visit www.icpi.org/picpcourse for more information on who is sponsoring courses, dates and locations.

Guide Construction Specification

SECTION 32 14 13.19
PERMEABLE INTERLOCKING CONCRETE PAVEMENT

(1995 MasterFormat Section 02795)

Note: This guide specification for U.S. applications describes construction of permeable interlocking concrete pavers on a permeable, open-graded crushed stone bedding layer (typically ASTM No. 8 stone). This 2 in. (50 mm) layer is placed over an open-graded base (typically ASTM No. 57 stone no greater than 4 in. or 100 mm thick) and a subbase (typically ASTM No. 2 stone or similar sized material). The pavers and bedding layer are placed over an open-graded crushed stone base with exfiltration to the soil subgrade. In low infiltration soils or installations with impermeable liners, some or all drainage is directed to an outlet via perforated drain pipes in the subbase. While this guide specification does not cover excavation, liners and drain pipes; notes are provided on these aspects.

The text must be edited to suit specific project requirements. It should be reviewed by a qualified civil or geotechnical engineer, or landscape architect familiar with the site conditions. Edit this specification term as necessary to identify the design professional in the General Conditions of the Contract.

PART 1 GENERAL

1.01 SUMMARY

    A. Section Includes
        1. Permeable interlocking concrete pavers.
        2. Crushed stone bedding material.
        3. Open-graded subbase aggregate.
        4. Open-graded base aggregate.
        5. Bedding and joint/opening filler materials.
        6. Edge restraints.
        7. [Geotextiles].
    B. Related Sections
        1. Section [_____]: Curbs.
        2. Section [_____]: [Stabilized] aggregate base.
        3. Section [_____]: [PVC] Drainage pipes.
        4. Section [_____]: Impermeable liner.
        5. Section [_____]: Edge restraints.
        6. Section [_____]: Drainage pipes and appurtenances.
        7. Section [_____]: Earthworks/excavation/soil compaction.

1.02 REFERENCES

    A. American Society for Testing and Materials (ASTM)
        1. C 131, Standard Test Method for Resistance to Degradation of Small-Size Coarse Aggregate by Abrasion and Impact in the Los Angeles Machine.
        2. C 136, Method for Sieve Analysis for Fine and Coarse Aggregate.
        3. C 140, Standard Test Methods for Sampling and Testing Concrete Masonry Units and Related Units.

4. D 448, Standard Classification for Sizes of Aggregate for Road and Bridge Construction.
5. C 936, Standard Specification for Solid Interlocking Concrete Paving Units.
6. C 979, Specification for Pigments for Integrally Colored Concrete.
7. D 698, Test Methods for Moisture Density Relations of Soil and Soil Aggregate Mixtures Using a 5.5-lb (2.49 kg) Rammer and 12 in. (305 mm) drop.
8. D 1557, Test Methods for Moisture Density Relations of Soil and Soil Aggregate Mixtures Using a 10-lb (4.54 kg) Rammer and 18 in. (457 mm) drop.
9. D 1883, Test Method for California Bearing Ratio of Laboratory-Compacted Soils.
10. ASTM D 2922 Standard Test Methods for Density of Soil and Soil-Aggregate In-Place by Nuclear Methods (Shallow Depth).
11. D 4254, Standard Test Methods for Minimum Index Density and Unit Weight of Soils and Calculation of Relative Density.

B. Interlocking Concrete Pavement Institute (ICPI)
1. Permeable Interlocking Concrete Pavement manual (latest edition).
2. Permeable Design Pro software for hydrologic and structural design

1.03 SUBMITTALS

A. In accordance with Conditions of the Contract and Division 1 Submittal Procedures Section.
B. Paver manufacturer's/installation subcontractor's drawings and details: Indicate perimeter conditions, junction with other materials, expansion and control joints, paver [layout,] [patterns,] [color arrangement,] installation [and setting] details. Indicate layout, pattern and relationship of paving joints to fixtures, and project formed details.
C. Minimum 3 lb (2 kg) samples of subbase, base and bedding aggregate materials.
D. Sieve analysis of aggregates for subbase, base and bedding materials per ASTM C 136.
E. Project specific or producer/manufacturer source test results for void ratio and bulk density of the base and subbase aggregates.
F. Soils report indicating density test reports, classification, and infiltration rate measured on-site under compacted conditions, and suitability for the intended project.
G. Erosion and sediment control plan.
H. [Stormwater management (quality and quantity) calculations; structural analysis for vehicular applications] using ICPI Permeable Interlocking Concrete Pavements manual, Permeable Design Pro or [specify] design methods and models.
I. Permeable concrete pavers:
1. Paver manufacturer's catalog sheets with product specifications.
2. [Four] representative full-size samples of each paver type, thickness, color, and finish. Submit samples indicating the range of color expected in the finished installation.
3. Accepted samples become the standard of acceptance for the work of this Section.
4. Laboratory test reports certifying compliance of the concrete pavers with ASTM C 936.
5. Manufacturer's certification of concrete pavers by ICPI as having met applicable ASTM standards.
6. Manufacturers' material safety data sheets for the safe handling of the specified paving materials and other products specified herein.
7. Paver manufacturer's written quality control procedures including representative samples of production record keeping that ensure conformance of paving products to the product specifications.
J. Paver Installation Subcontractor:
1. Demonstrate that job foremen on the project have a current certificate from the Interlocking Concrete Pavement Institute Concrete Paver Installer Certification program and a record of completion from the PICP Specialist Course.

2. Job references from projects of a similar size and complexity. Provide Owner/Client/General Contractor names, postal address, phone, fax, and email address.
3. Written Method Statement and Quality Control Plan that describes material staging and flow, paving direction and installation procedures, including representative reporting forms that ensure conformance to the project specifications.

1.04 QUALITY ASSURANCE

A. Paver Installation Subcontractor Qualifications:
1. Utilize an installer having successfully completed concrete paver installation similar in design, material and extent indicated on this project.
2. Utilize an installer with job foremen holding a current certificate from the Interlocking Concrete Pavement Institute Concrete Paver Installer Certification program and having a certificate of completion from the PICP Specialist Course.
B. Regulatory Requirements and Approvals: [Specify applicable licensing, bonding or other requirements of regulatory agencies.].
C. Review the manufacturers' quality control plan, paver installation subcontractor's Method Statement and Quality Control Plan with a pre-construction meeting of representatives from the manufacturer, paver installation subcontractor, general contractor, engineer and/or owner's representative.
D. Mock-Ups:
1. Install a 10 ft x 10 ft (3 x 3 m) paver area.

Note: Mechanized installations may require a larger mock up area. Consult with the paver installation contractor on the size of the mock up.

2. Use this area to determine surcharge of the bedding layer, joint sizes, and lines, laying pattern, color and texture of the job.
3. This area will be used as the standard by which the work will be judged.
4. Subject to acceptance by owner, mock-up may be retained as part of finished work.
5. If mock-up is not retained, remove and properly dispose of mock-up.

1.05 DELIVERY, STORAGE, AND HANDLING

A. General: Comply with Division 1 Product Requirement Section.
B. Comply with manufacturer's ordering instructions and lead-time requirements to avoid construction delays.
C. Delivery: Deliver materials in manufacturer's original, unopened, undamaged container packaging with identification tags intact on each paver bundle.
1. Coordinate delivery and paving schedule to minimize interference with normal use of buildings adjacent to paving.
2. Deliver concrete pavers to the site in steel banded, plastic banded, or plastic wrapped cubes capable of transfer by forklift or clamp lift.
3. Unload pavers at job site in such a manner that no damage occurs to the product or existing construction
D Storage and Protection: Store materials in protected area such that they are kept free from mud, dirt, and other foreign materials.

1.06 ENVIRONMENTAL REQUIREMENTS

A. Do not install in conditions where conformance to these specifications cannot be achieved or is not practical.
B. Do not install frozen bedding materials.

1.07 MAINTENANCE MATERIALS

    A. Extra materials: Provide [Specify area] [Specify percentage] [Number of pallets] additional paver material for use by owner for maintenance and repair.

    B. Pavers shall be from the same production run as installed materials.

    C. Store paver materials in [location] for maintenance.

PART 2 PRODUCTS

Note: Some projects may include permeable and solid interlocking concrete pavements. Specify each product as required.

    A. Manufacturer: [Specify ICPI member manufacturer name.].

        1. Contact: [Specify ICPI member manufacturer contact information.].

    B. Permeable Interlocking Concrete Paver Units:

        1. Paver Type: [Specify name of product group, family, series, etc.].

            a. Material Standard: Comply with ASTM C 936.

            b. Color [and finish]: [Specify color.] [Specify finish].

            c. Color Pigment Material Standard: Comply with ASTM C 979.

Note: Concrete pavers may have spacer bars on each unit. Spacer bars are recommended for mechanically installed pavers. Manually installed pavers may be installed with or without spacer bars. Verify with manufacturers that overall dimensions do not include spacer bars.

            d. Size: [Specify.] inches [({Specify.}mm)] x [Specify.] inches [({Specify}mm)] x [Specify.] inches [({Specify.} mm)] thick.

2.02 PRODUCT SUBSTITUTIONS

    A. Substitutions: Permitted for gradations for crushed stone jointing material, base and subbase materials. All substitutions shall be approved in writing by the project engineer.

2.03 CRUSHED STONE FILLER, BEDDING, BASE AND SUBBASE

    A. Crushed stone with 90% fractured faces, LA Abrasion < 40 per ASTM C 131, minimum CBR of 80% per ASTM D 1883.

    B. Do not use rounded river gravel for vehicular applications.

    C. All stone materials shall have equal to or less than 2% passing the No. 200 (0.075 mm) sieve.

    D. Joint/opening filler, bedding, base and subbase: conforming to ASTM D 448 gradation as shown in Tables 1, 2 and 3 below:

Note: ASTM No. 89 or ASTM No. 9 stone may be used to fill pavers with narrow joints.

Table 1. ASTM No. 8 Grading Requirements

Bedding and Joint/Opening Filler	
Sieve Size	**Percent Passing**
12.5 mm (1/2 in.)	100
9.5 mm (3/8 in.)	85 to 100
4.75 mm (No. 4)	10 to 30
2.36 mm (No. 8)	0 to 10
1.16 mm (No. 16)	0 to 5

Table 2. ASTM No. 57 Base Grading Requirements

Sieve Size	Percent Passing
37.5 mm (1½ in.)	100
25 mm (1 in.)	95 to 100
12.5 mm (½ in.)	25 to 60
4.75 mm (No. 4)	0 to 10
2.36 mm (No. 8)	0 to 5

Table 3. ASTM No. 2 Subbase Grading Requirements

Sieve Size	Percent Passing
75 mm (3 in.)	100
63 mm (2½ in.)	90 to 100
50 mm (2 in.)	35 to 70
37.5 mm (1½ in.)	0 to 15
19 mm (¾ in.)	0 to 5

2.04 ACCESSORIES

A.   Provide accessory materials as follows:

Note: Curbs will typically be cast-in-place concrete or precast concrete or cut stone set in concrete haunches. Concrete curbs may be specified in another Section. Do not use plastic edging with steel spikes to restrain the paving units for vehicular applications.

1.   Edge Restraints
  a.   Manufacturer: [Specify manufacturer.].
  b.   Material: [Precast concrete] [Cut stone] [Concrete].
  b.   Material Standard: [Specify material standard.].

Note: See ICPI publication, Permeable Interlocking Concrete Pavements for guidance on geotextile selection. Geotextile use is optional.

2.   Geotextile Fabric:
  a.   Material Type and Description: [Specify material type and description.].
  b.   Material Standard: [Specify material standard.].
  c.   Manufacturer: [Acceptable to interlocking concrete paver manufacturer]]

PART 3 EXECUTION

3.01 QUALIFIED INSTALLERS

A. [Specify approved paver installation subcontractors that meet criteria in 1.04.].

Note: Curbs are typically cast-in-place concrete or precast concrete or cut stone set in concrete haunches. Concrete curbs may be specified in another Section. Do not use plastic edging with steel spikes to restrain the paving units for vehicular applications.

Note: The elevations and surface tolerance of the soil subgrade determine the final surface elevations of concrete pavers. The paver installation contractor cannot correct deficiencies excavation and grading of the soil subgrade with additional bedding materials. Therefore, the surface elevations of the soil subgrade should be checked and accepted by the General Contractor or designated party, with written certification presented to the paver installation subcontractor prior to starting work.

3.02 EXAMINATION

A. Acceptance of Site Verification of Conditions:
    1. General Contractor shall inspect, accept and certify in writing to the paver installation subcontractor that site conditions meet specifications for the following items prior to installation of interlocking concrete pavers.

Note: Compaction of the soil subgrade is optional and should be determined by the project engineer. If the soil subgrade requires compaction, compact to a minimum of 95% standard Proctor density per ASTM C 698. Compacted soil density and moisture should be checked in the field with a nuclear density gauge or other test methods for compliance to specifications. Stabilization of the soil and/or base material may be necessary with weak or continually saturated soils, or when subject to high wheel loads. Compaction will reduce the permeability of soils. If soil compaction is necessary, reduced infiltration may require drain pipes within the open-graded subbase to conform to local storm drainage requirements.

        a. Verify that subgrade preparation, compacted density and elevations conform to specified requirements.
        b. Provide written density test results for soil subgrade to the Owner, General Contractor and paver installation subcontractor.
        c. Verify location, type, and elevations of edge restraints, [concrete collars around] utility structures, and drainage pipes and inlets.
    2. Do not proceed with installation of bedding and interlocking concrete pavers until subgrade soil conditions are corrected by the General Contractor or designated subcontractor.

3.03 PREPARATION

A. Verify that the soil subgrade is free from standing water.
B. Stockpile joint/opening filler, base and subbase materials such that they are free from standing water, uniformly graded, free of any organic material or sediment, debris, and ready for placement.
C. Edge Restraint Preparation:
    1. Install edge restraints per the drawings [at the indicated elevations].

3.04 INSTALLATION

Note: The minimum slope of the soil subgrade is typically 0.5%. Actual slope of soil subgrade will depend on the drainage design and exfiltration type. All drain pipes, observation wells, overflow pipes, and (if applicable) geotextiles, berms, baffles and impermeable liner should be in place per the drawings prior to or during placement of the subbase and base, depending on their location. Care must be taken not to damage drainpipes during compaction and paving. No mud or sediment can be left on the base or bedding aggregates. If they are contaminated, they must be removed and replaced with clean materials. Base/subbase thicknesses and drainage should be determined using ICPI's Permeable Interlocking Concrete Pavements manual and Permeable Design Pro software.

- A. General
    1. Any excess thickness of soil applied over the excavated soil subgrade to trap sediment from adjacent construction activities shall be removed before application of the [geotextile] and subbase materials.
    2. Keep area where pavement is to be constructed free from sediment during entire job. [Geotextiles] Base and bedding materials contaminated with sediment shall be removed and replaced with clean materials.
    3. Do not damage drainpipes, overflow pipes, observation wells, or any inlets and other drainage appurtenances during installation. Report any damage immediately to the project engineer.
- B. Geotextiles
    1. Place on [bottom and] sides of soil subgrade. Secure in place to prevent wrinkling from vehicle tires and tracks.
    2. Overlap a minimum of [0.3 m (12 in.)] [0.6 m (24 in.)] in the direction of drainage.
- C. Open-graded subbase and base
    1. Moisten, spread and compact the ASTM No. 2 subbase in 6 in. (150 mm) lifts [without wrinkling or folding the geotextile. Place subbase to protect geotextile from wrinkling under equipment tires and tracks.]
    2. For each lift, make at least two passes in the vibratory mode then at least two in the static mode with a minimum 10 t (10 T) vibratory roller until there is no visible movement of the ASTM No. 2 stone. Do not crush aggregate with the roller.
    3. The surface tolerance of the compacted ASTM No. 2 subbase shall be ±2¹/₂ in. (± 65mm) over a 10 ft (3 m) straightedge.
    4. Moisten, spread and compact the ASTM No. 57 base layer in one 4 in. (100 mm) thick lift. On this layer, make at least two passes in the vibratory mode then at least two in the static mode with a minimum 10 t (10 T) vibratory roller until there is no visible movement of the ASTM No. 57 stone. Do not crush aggregate with the roller.

Note: At the option of the specifier, this supplemental test method noted below can be used to establish a consistent methodology for in-situ density data collection of open-graded aggregate base layer (typically ASTM No. 57 stone). This test method can assist contractors in reaching adequate job site compaction and offer an additional level of confidence for the project owner and designer. This test method is appropriate for pavement subject to consistent vehicular traffic such as parking lots and roads. It is not needed for pedestrian areas and residential driveways. The specifier should consider using state/provincial DOT specifications in lieu of these.

    5. Use part of the compacted base area as a control strip for density testing by the [Testing Company].

a. The [Testing Company] shall supply nuclear moisture/density gauges and ancillary equipment required to conduct density and moisture content measurements for compaction of the ASTM No. 57 aggregate drainage layer. Qualified testing laboratory operators/gauges may conduct compaction testing. Each gauge operator shall be trained in the safe operation, transportation and handling of the gauge. The registered owner of the gauge shall have and maintain a valid Radioisotope License for each gauge.

b. Each gauge shall have been calibrated within the last 12 months, either by the manufacturer or other qualified agent, against certified density and moisture reference blocks. The density standard count and the moisture standard count shall be within 2 percent and 4 percent respectively, of the most recent calibration values. A certificate of calibration for each gauge shall accompany each gauge.

6. Target Density

a. Determine a target density on the control strip during under the following conditions: (1) after initial placement and compaction of the base aggregate layer (2) when there is a perceptible change in the appearance or gradation of the aggregate, (3) when there is a change in the source of aggregate.

b. Test field density according to ASTM D 2922 Standard Test Methods for Density of Soil and Soil-Aggregate In-Place by Nuclear Methods (shallow Depth). Field density tests shall be performed on compacted base materials to determine within acceptable limits of a target density.

7. Control Strip

a. The Testing Company shall construct a control strip for the determination of a target density consisting of a single uniform lift as specified in the contract documents, but not more than 4 in. (100 mm) thick and covering approximately 600 yd² (500 m²) in area. No testing shall be performed within 10 ft (3 m) from any unrestrained outside edge of the work area. The control strip may be incorporated into the project upon acceptance of density measurements by the Testing Company.

b. During construction of the control strip, the surface of the aggregate shall be visibly moist and maintained as such throughout construction and compaction.

c. After initial placement of the aggregate base material, the compaction equipment shall make two passes over the entire surface of the control strip. Field densities and field moisture contents, using the backscatter/indirect method, shall be determined at five randomly selected locations at least 15 ft (5 m) apart. The dry density and moisture content shall be calculated for each of these locations and the averages shall be used as initial values. The maximum compacted thickness of the aggregate base layer measured for density shall be 4 in. (100 mm).

d. The compaction equipment shall then make two additional passes over the entire surface of the control strip. After compaction, three separate, random field density and moisture content determinations shall be made, using the backscatter/indirect method, and a new average dry density and moisture content shall be calculated.

e. If the new average dry density exceeds the previous value by more than 1.2 pcf (20 kg/m³) then two additional passes of the equipment shall be carried out as described above. If the new average dry density does not exceed the previous value by more than 1.2 pcf (20 kg/m³), then compaction of the control strip will be considered satisfactory and complete.

f. Upon satisfactory completion of the control strip, an additional seven (7) field density and moisture tests, using the backscatter/indirect method, shall be taken at random

locations and the dry density and moisture content values shall be determined. The final dry density and moisture content of the control strip shall be the average of these seven values plus the three most recent values obtained upon completion.

8. Compaction Equipment
   a. Use a smooth dual or single smooth drum, minimum 10 ton (10 T) vibratory roller or a minimum 13,500 lbf (60 kN) centrifugal force, reversible vibratory plate compactor that provides maximum compaction force without crushing the aggregate base.

9. Test Report
   a. The test report shall include the following:
      1) Project description.
      2) Sketch of test area and test locations.
      3) Aggregate type and layer thicknesses.
      4) Aggregate characteristic properties: gradation, void ratio, bulk density.
      5) Compaction equipment type and weight.
      6) Static or vibratory compaction.
      7) Number of passes of the compaction equipment.
      8) Test number and location.
      9) Individual and average field wet density, moisture content, and dry density values determined after each compaction operation in accordance with ASTM D 2922 *Standard Test Methods for Density of Soil and Soil-Aggregate In-Place by Nuclear Methods (Shallow Depth)*.
      10) Calculation of target density.

D. The surface tolerance the compacted ASTM No. 57 base should not deviate more than. ±1 in. (25 mm) over a 10 ft (3 m) straightedge.

Note: As an alternative test method, in-place density of the base aggregate may be checked per ASTM D 4254. Compacted density should be 95% of the laboratory index density established for the base layer.

E. Bedding layer
   1. Moisten, spread and screed the ASTM No. 8 stone bedding material.
   2. Fill voids left by removed screed rails with ASTM No. 8 stone.
   3. The surface tolerance of the screeded ASTM No. 8 bedding layer shall be ±3/8 in (10 mm) over a 10 ft (3 m) straightedge.
   4. Do not subject screeded bedding material to any pedestrian or vehicular traffic before paving unit installation begins.

F. Permeable interlocking concrete pavers and joint/opening fill material
   1. Lay the paving units in the pattern(s) and joint widths shown on the drawings. Maintain straight pattern lines.
   2. Fill gaps at the edges of the paved area with cut units. Cut pavers subject to tire traffic shall be no smaller than 1/3 of a whole unit.
   3. Cut pavers and place along the edges with a [double-bladed splitter or] masonry saw.
   4. Fill the openings and joints with [ASTM No. 8] stone.

Note: Some paver joint widths may be narrow and not accept most of the ASTM No. 8 stone. Use joint material that will fill joints such as washed ASTM No. 89 or ASTM No. 9 stone.

   5. Remove excess aggregate on the surface by sweeping pavers clean.

6   Compact and seat the pavers into the bedding material using a low-amplitude, 75-90 Hz plate compactor capable of at least 5,000 lbf (22 kN) centrifugal compaction force. This will require at least two passes with the plate compactor.

7. Do not compact within 6 ft (2 m) of the unrestrained edges of the paving units.

8. Apply additional aggregate to the openings and joints if needed, filling them completely. Remove excess aggregate by sweeping then compact the pavers. This will require at least two passes with the plate compactor.

9. All pavers within 6 ft (2 m) of the laying face must be left fully compacted at the completion of each day.

10. The final surface tolerance of compacted pavers shall not deviate more than ±3/8 (10 mm) under a 10 ft (3 m) long straightedge.

11. The surface elevation of pavers shall be 1/8 to 1/4 in. (3 to 6 mm) above adjacent drainage inlets, concrete collars or channels.

3.05 FIELD QUALITY CONTROL

A. After sweeping the surface clean, check final elevations for conformance to the drawings.

B. Lippage: No greater than 1/8 in. (3 mm) difference in height between adjacent pavers.

Note: The surface of the pavers may be 1/8 to 1/4 in. (3 to 6 mm) above the final elevations after compaction. This helps compensate for possible minor settling normal to pavements.

C. The surface elevation of pavers shall be 1/8 to 1/4 in. (3 to 6 mm) above adjacent drainage inlets, concrete collars or channels.

D. Bond lines for paver courses: ±1/2 in. (±15 mm) over a 50 ft (15 m) string line.

E. The PICP installation contractor shall return to site after 6 months from the completion of the work and provide the following as required: fill paver joints with stones, replace broken or cracked pavers, and re-level settled pavers to specified elevations. Any rectification work shall be considered part of original bid price and with no additional compensation.

3.06 PROTECTION

A. After work in this section is complete, the General Contractor shall be responsible for protecting work from sediment deposition and damage due to subsequent construction activity on the site.

END OF SECTION

Section 5. Maintenance

This Section provides maintenance guidelines and an in-service inspection checklist for municipalities and project owners. Also included is a model maintenance agreement that can be used between a project owner who has installed PICP and the local municipality to help ensure maintenance. As an additional resource, a model zoning ordinance is provided that can be used as a template or starting point for a city enabling PICP use by property owners. A growing number of municipalities provide financial incentives to homeowners and commercial developers for using permeable pavements. The cost to the municipality can be less than upsizing storm sewer systems operating at their capacity.

Like all permeable pavements, PICP surfaces can become clogged with sediment over time, thereby slowing its infiltration rate. The rate of sedimentation depends on the amount of traffic and other sources that wash sediment into the joints, base and soil. Sources can be eroding soil, leaves, mulch, and sediment deposited from vehicles. PICP streets and parking lots can be cleaned with municipal street cleaning equipment and snow plows. Many municipal streets receive cleaning a few times annually and that can be sufficient to control the buildup of sediment in PICP joints. The following provides guidelines on managing surface infiltration based on research and experience.

Traffic and sediment sources vary with every PICP project. Regular surface cleaning will help maintain a high surface infiltration rate and keep out vegetation. ICPI recommends inspection and cleaning once or twice in the first year of service and adjusting cleaning intervals higher or lower as needed. Cleaning can be done with vacuuming sweeping equipment such a regenerative air vacuum sweepers. Adjustments to the vacuum force likely will be required to minimize removal of stones from the openings. Sweeping alone is not effective since vacuuming removes much of the sediment. Sweeping only moves it from one place to another.

When monitoring PICP, there are two means to determining if the surface is infiltrating:

> (1) Observe drainage immediately after a heavy rainstorm for standing water; or
> (2) Conduct surface infiltration tests using ASTM C1701 (ASTM 2009).

The test ASTM method was originally developed Bean (2007) for evaluating the surface infiltration of PICP, concrete grid pavement and pervious concrete. The test method was refined and adopted by ASTM for use on pervious concrete and successfully used on PICP. If there is a substantial area or areas of standing water on PICP after a storm, or should the measured surface infiltration rate using C1701 fall below the design infiltration rate, the surface should be cleaned with vacuum equipment. The type and use of this equipment will be covered later. ICPI recommends cleaning if the tested surface infiltration rate falls below 10 in./hr (250 mm/hr).

Figure 5-1 illustrates C1701 test apparatus for measuring PICP surface infiltration rate. A five gallon (20 l) bucket of water is slowly poured into a 12 in. (300 mm) ring secured to the pavers with plumber's putty. The putty creates a waterproof seal and is placed in the joints (upon removal of jointing stone) directly under the ring to direct water downward. The water inflow rate does not exceed a head of 3/8 in. (10 mm) while being timed with a stopwatch. The surface infiltration rate is calculated using formulas in the test method.

Figure 5-1. Test apparatus on PICP for measuring surface infiltration rate per ASTM C1701.

Some PICP surfaces do not require surface cleaning for years because they maintain adequate infiltration. This was demonstrated at a PICP parking lot in an arboretum in suburban Chicago in 2009. The seven year-old, 500-car parking lot had been infiltrating rainfall adequately. The demonstration confirmed what other researchers have found, i.e., the small aggregates in the joints have a dual function: (1) they receive sediment and thereby reducing surface infiltration over time; and (2) the aggregates provide a first line of defense by trapping sediment and preventing it from entering the base and soil subgrade. (See pages 20–21 for a literature review.) Trapping sediment in joints can continue for years and at some point they may require cleaning. As noted above, that point is decided by observation or by surface infiltration testing.

The arboretum PICP parking lot received much car and bus traffic, as well as sand and deicing materials in the winter. The surface was not cleaned since its construction in 2002. Pavers and jointing material were removed in a heavily trafficked delivery area to observe the path and penetration of sediments in the joints. Figure 5-2 shows that much of the sediment was trapped in the first ½ to inch (12 to 25 mm) of the openings. The pavers and jointing material were removed and there was no sediment visible on the bedding material or in the ASTM No. 57 stone base as shown in Figure 5-3. This demonstrated the surface sediment trapping capability of this PICP installation and this pattern has been observed on other installations.

Since PICP is trapping sediment in the jointing aggregates, some cases with low infiltration will require their removal and replacement. This procedure was demonstrated at the arboretum parking lot with a vacuum machine capable of removing the stones and sediment captured in the joints. The vacuum machine was adjusted to so that only the top inch (25 mm) of stones and sediment were removed (Figures 5-4 and 5-5). This substantially increased the surface infiltration rate based on observing differences in the rate of water poured on and penetrating undisturbed and restored surfaces. Stones were spread

Figure 5-2. Concrete pavers are removed from a seven year-old PICP parking lot. Note the accumulation of sediment in the square-shape openings in the pavers.

Figure 5-3. No visible sediment was found in the bedding or within the ASTM No. 57 stone base in this heavily trafficked area.

and swept into the openings thereby refilling them to their original condition. Figure 5-6 shows the joints prior to vacuuming and Figure 5-7 shows the cleaned joints filled with fresh stone.

Besides this demonstration, research by Gerrits (2002) Bean (2004) and Chopra (2010) have shown that removal of sediment in the openings increases surface infiltration rates. A significant maintenance advantage of PICP over pervious monolithic pavements is the ability to restore heavily clogged joints in PICP. This has been observed by Chopra in evaluating the ability to clean highly clogged permeable pavements, and obtaining favorable results with PICP. Researchers at the University of Minnesota noted that sediment penetrating over ¼ in. (6 mm) in pervious concrete was impossible to remove with vacuum equipment (Vancura 2010).

Winter maintenance—Snow can be plowed from pavers as with any other pavement. Since deicing salts will infiltrate into the base and soil, they should be applied sparingly, as they can accumulate in the soil subgrade. Research at the Toronto and Region Conservation Authority (Van Seters 2007) indicates that PICPs require less deicing salt than asphalt pavements, since permeable pavement remains warmer throughout the winter.

Sand should not be applied on the PICP for traction, as it will accelerate surface clogging. If traction is required, ASTM No. 8, 89 or 9 stone (or similar) should be used. If sand is used, PICP surface should be

Figures 5-4 and 5-5. The vacuum machine removed the top inch (25 mm) of sediment and jointing stone.

Figures 5-6 and 5-7. Before and after cleaning with fresh stones swept into the joints

vacuumed in the spring to reduce the risk of decreased surface infiltration.

Many years of experience and monitoring have demonstrated that PICP does not heave when frozen. This is evidenced by many PICP projects in Chicago, Minneapolis and Toronto remaining stable during freezing and thawing climates. This is due to the following factors:

- The pavement base and saturated soil subgrade drains prior to freezing;

- The air in the aggregate voids provides some insulating effect in slowing the movement of freezing temperatures toward the soil subgrade;

- The moisture and earth provide some heat to delay freezing of the soil subgrade and base/subbase such that both can drain prior to freezing; and

- Should water freeze in the base or subbase, there is sufficient space in the aggregate voids for the frozen water to expand as it freezes and avoid heaving.

A benefit of all permeable pavements is snow remaining after plowing can melt and infiltrate into the surface when temperatures rise, thereby reducing or eliminating re-freezing at night and ice hazards. This condition also reduces deicing salts and potential legal liability from injury claims due to falls.

Cracked or damaged paving units, bedding and base can be removed and replaced, and such repairs can be done in the winter provided that aggregate materials are not frozen. This provides a maintenance advantage over site-formed materials that require above freezing temperatures for placement, as well as difficulty in finding a wintertime source of material supply.

Reinstatement—An advantage of PICP is that they can be removed for access to underground utilities. The following steps are recommended:

1. Pavers are removed, cleaned and stacked for reinstatement. If the PICP installation has some age to it, the pavers will require removal of dirt that typically accumulates in the stone filled openings at the surface. Undisturbed pavers can be secured with wood or metal frame as show in Figure 5-8.

2. The bedding material (typically ASTM No. 8 stone) should be removed and disposed of, then replaced with fresh stones. The reason for its disposal is that it is mixed with ASTM No. 57 base stone and it cannot be reinstated with it.

3. The ASTM No. 57 base layer (typically 4 in. or 100 mm thick) can be removed and stored for reinstatement as well as the ASTM No. 2 subbase material. Store in a place where the aggregates will remain clean. All dirty/contaminated aggregates should be replaced with clean stone.

4. Repairs can then be made to the utility pipe or box that is slightly above, on or in the soil subgrade.

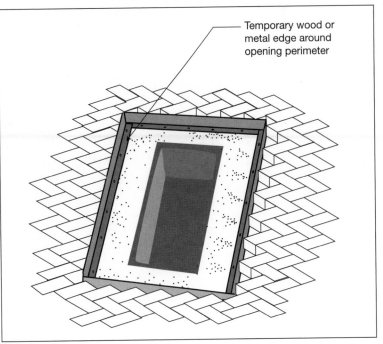

Temporary wood or metal edge around opening perimeter

Figure 5-8. Restraining undisturbed pavers with a wood or metal frame can save time when reinstating concrete pavers.

5. Flowable concrete fill (200 to 500 psi or 1.4 to 3.5 MPa) should be used to support repaired utilities. This material is also known as controlled low-strength material or CLSM. Flowable fill is needed because open-graded base cannot adequately fill under pipes or boxes, nor can it be compacted in these places. Many cities use flowable fill for utility repairs and have material and installation specifications.

6. A minimum 4 in. (100 mm) layer of flowable concrete fill should be cover the pipe or box. Then the subbase can be reinstated around it. Flowable fill will likely seep into the ASTM No. 2 stone, so there needs to be a barrier to stop it. That can be plastic sheets or geotextile. Flowable fill takes a few hours to stiffen. After 24 hours, the subbase stone should be reinstated and compacted. There should be at least 12 in. (300 mm) distance between the top of the flowable fill and the bottom of the plate compactor. The compactor force should be 13,500 lbf (60 kN).

7. The ASTM No. 57 base is reinstated and compacted.

8. New ASTM No. 2 stone is placed and screeded. Sometime it helps to remove a few courses of undisturbed pavers so the new and existing bedding layers can be screeded together.

9. Pavers are reinstated, joints filled and compacted. The pavers should be at least one inch (25 mm) above the surrounding undisturbed pavers prior to compaction. They will compact down and probably settle a bit after compaction as all flexible pavements. Likewise, the same units can be reinstated after repairs to the base, drain pipes, liners or underground utilities.

While not typically done, sealers can be applied to the pavers. Overflow onto the aggregates is avoided by using a roller. Such sealers can enhance appearance while making stains easier to remove.

As noted in Section 4, PICP is sometimes constructed with an observation well. The well is typically a 4 to 6 in. (100 to 150 mm) diameter perforated pipe with a screw cap just slightly below the surface of the pavers that can be removed to observe the exfiltration rate. The cap should lock and be vandal-resistant. The depth to the soil subgrade should be marked on the lid. The observation well is located in the furthest down-slope area within 3 ft (1 m) from the pavement edge. Figure 5-9 shows an observation well as a parking lot at a U.S. Army base in Georgia. The top of the pipe can also be placed under the pavers. This hides the cap from vandals and a few pavers can be removed to access the well cap and reinstated.

Figure 5-9. A PVC pipe with a screw cap serves as an observation well on PICP parking lot at a U.S. Army base in Georgia.

Long Term Performance and Maintenance Agreements

When carefully constructed and regularly maintained, PICP can provide as much as 40 years of service. Their structural service life is measured by the extent of rutting of the base/subbase or soil subgrade. Their hydrologic service life is measured by the extent to which they continue infiltrating and storing runoff.

At some point later in the life of the pavement, PICP may no longer store the required amount of water to control runoff. In such cases, the pavers will need to be removed, the base materials and geotextile removed and replaced. Clogged or broken drain pipes will require replacement. Once new materials are in place, the same pavers can be reinstated. Removal and replacement of the base and pavers is an expensive operation. Other lower-cost alternatives may be possible such as cleaning or replacing selected clogged pipes (rather than the entire base and pipe system) or diverting drainage to another BMP. Regular maintenance and inspection are important to tracking drainage performance, sources of problems, and deciding on possible solutions.

The PICP owner plays a key role in maintenance and successful long-term performance of permeable interlocking concrete pavements. The owner should have long-term ownership and oversight of the property and be aware of maintenance requirements. A growing trend to ensure oversight is a maintenance agreement. It is typically between the property owner and the local city or county, and the agreement is recorded and attached to the deed for the property.

The model agreement presented below is applicable to many BMPs. It can be edited to suit local situations and customized for PICP maintenance. A list of maintenance items should be an attachment to this agreement, as well as an inspection schedule. This list of items to be inspected can be developed from the in-service inspection check-list in this section as well as from requirements established by the local government. A growing number of local governments are creating databases in which to place BMP inspection data. This provides continual documentation of care and performance. As an alternative to municipal-landowner maintenance agreements is the use of performance bonds. The owner typically posts a bond or promise, often as a bank letter of credit, that the municipality can draw money from if written maintenance criteria are not met. Other municipalities may have the right to enter private property, conduct maintenance on BMPs and invoice the land owner or attach a tax lien on the property.

Model Maintenance Agreement

This Maintenance Agreement made this _____ day of _____, [year], by and between [property owner/s], hereinafter referred to as "Grantor," and the [city/county of state/province] hereinafter referred to as the "[city/county]."

WITNESSETH

WHEREAS, the [city/county] is authorized ad required to regulate and control disposition of storm and surface waters within the [city/county/watershed] as set forth by [city/county] [state/provincial] ordinances; and

WHEREAS, the Grantor is the owner of a certain tract or parcel of land more particularly described as [legal description].

ALL THOSE certain lots, pieces or parcels of land, together with buildings and improvements thereon, and the appurtenances thereunto belonging, lying, situated and being in the [city/county] of [state/province] as shown on [tax maps/subdivisions plats numbers and names], duly recorded in the Clerk's Office of the [court] of [city/county] in Deed Book or Plat Book [number] at page [number] reference to which the plat is hereby made for a more particular description thereof.

It being the said property conveyed unto the Grantor herein by deed dated _____ from _____ and recorded in the Clerk's office aforesaid in Deed Book_____ at Page _____ such property being hereinafter referred to as "the property."

WHEREAS, the Grantor desires to construct certain improvements on the property which will alter existing storm and surface water conditions on the property and adjacent lands; and

WHEREAS, in order to accommodate and regulate these anticipated changes in existing storm and surface water flow conditions, the Grantor, its heirs and assigns, desire to build and maintain at their expense a storm and surface water management facility and system [more particularly described as a permeable interlocking concrete pavement]. This is shown on plat titled _____ and dated _____; and

WHEREAS, the [city/county] has reviewed and approved these plans subject to the execution of this agreement;

NOW THEREFORE, in consideration of the benefit received by the Grantor, its heirs and assigns, and as a result of the [city/county] approval of its plans, the Grantor, it heirs and assigns, with full authority to execute deeds, deeds of trust, other covenants and all rights, title and interest in the property described above hereby covenant with the [city/county] as follows:

1. Grantor, its heirs and assigns shall construct and perpetually maintain, at its sole expense, the above referenced permeable interlocking concrete pavement [storm and surface management facility and system] in strict accordance with the plan approval granted by the [city/county].

2. Grantor, its heirs and assigns shall, at its sole expense, make such changes or modifications to the permeable interlocking concrete pavement [storm drainage facility and system]. Changes or modifications may, in the [city's/county's] discretion, be determined necessary to ensure that the facility and system are property maintained and continues to operate as designed and approved.

3. The [city/county], it agents, employees and contractors shall have the perpetual right of ingress and egress over the property of the Grantor, its heirs assigns, and the right to inspect [at reasonable times and in a reasonable manner,] the permeable interlocking concrete pavement [storm drainage facility and system]. Inspection is in order to insure that the system is being properly maintained and is continuing to perform in an adequate manner. [Attachment A to this agreement provides a list of items to be inspected by the [city/county]].

4. The Grantor, its heirs and assigns agree that should it fail to correct any defects in the above described facility and system within [ten (10)] days from issuance of written notice, or shall fail to maintain the facility in accordance with the approved design standards and in accordance with the law and applicable regulations, or in the event of an emergency as determined by the [city/county] in its sole discretion, the [city/county] is authorized to enter the property to make all repairs, and to perform all maintenance, construction and reconstruction the [city/county] deems necessary. The [city/county] shall assess the Grantor, its heirs or assigns for the cost of the work, both direct and indirect, and applicable penalties. Said assessment shall be a lien against all properties described within this Maintenance Agreement and may be placed on the property tax bills of said properties and collected as ordinary taxes by the [city/county].

5. Grantor, its heirs and assigns shall indemnify, hold harmless and defend the [city/county] from and against any and all claims, demands, suit liabilities, losses, damages and payments, including attorney fees claimed or made against the [city/county] that are alleged or proven to result or arise from the Grantor, its heirs and covenant.

6. The Covenants contained herein shall run with the land and the Grantor, its heirs assigns further agree whenever the property shall be held, sold and conveyed, it shall be subject to the covenants stipulations, agreements and provisions of this Agreement, which shall apply to, bind all present and subsequent owners of the property described herein.

7. Grantor agrees to not transfer or assign responsibility.

8. The provisions of this Maintenance Agreement shall be severable and if any phase, clause, sentence or provision is declared unconstitutional, or the applicability of the Grantor, its heirs and assigns is held invalid, the remainder of this Covenant shall not be affected thereby.

9. The Maintenance Agreement shall be recorded at the Clerk's Office of the [court] of [city/county], [state/province] at the Grantor's, its heirs and assign's expense.

10. In the event that the [city/county] shall determine its sole discretion at any future time that the facility is no longer required, then the [city/county] shall at the request of the Grantor, its heirs and assigns execute a release of this Maintenance Agreement, which the Grantor, its heirs and assigns shall record, in the Clerk's Office at its expense.

IN WITNESS THEREOF, the Grantor has executed this Maintenance Agreement

On the _____ day of _____, [year].

By Officer/Authorized Agency

[State/Province] of:

[City/County] of :

To wit: The foregoing instrument was acknowledged before me this_____day of_____, [year], by _____

PICP Maintenance Checklist

This can be included in the above agreement or used separately to manage in-service PICP.

PICP In-service Inspection Checklist

❐ 1 to 2 times annually (typically spring/fall): vacuum surface, adjust vacuuming schedule per sediment loading and/or any sand deposits from winter

❐ Winter: Remove snow with standard plow/snow blowing equipment; monitor ice on surface for reduced salt use than typically used on impervious pavements

❐ As needed, indicated by water ponding on surface immediately after a storm (paver joints or openings severely loaded with sediment): test surface infiltration rate using ASTM C1701. Vacuum to remove surface sediment and soiled aggregate (typically 1/2 to 1 in. or 13-25 mm deep), refill joints with clean aggregate, sweep surface clean and test infiltration rate again per C1701 to minimum 50% increase or minimum 10 in./hr (250 mm/hr).

Annual Inspection

❐ Replenish aggregate in joints if more than 1/2 in. (13 mm) from chamfer bottoms on paver surfaces

❐ Inspect vegetation around PICP perimeter for cover & soil stability, repair/replant as needed

❐ Inspect and repair all paver surface deformations exceeding 1/2 in. (13 mm)

❐ Repair pavers offset by more than 1/4 in. (6 mm) above/below adjacent units or curbs, inlets etc.

❐ Replace cracked paver units impairing surface structural integrity

❐ Check drains outfalls for free flow of water and outflow from observation well after a major storm

Model Stormwater Ordinance

The following model stormwater ordinance gives local governments a start in developing a stormwater ordinance that includes PICP. The ordinance should be adjusted to accommodate local conditions.

Stormwater Management Using PICP (Community) Ordinance No. _____

(a) Purpose. The purpose of this Ordinance is to promote health, safety, and welfare within (community) and its watershed by minimizing the harms and maximizing the benefits, through provisions designed for allowance of permeable interlocking concrete pavement (PICP) as part of a stormwater management planning and implementation of stormwater goals for (Community). (Community) recognizes that stormwater runoff has been traditionally treated as a by-product of development and mainly from impervious surfaces (roofs and paving) to be disposed of quickly and efficiently. The result is typically increased flooding, degradation of surface and subsurface water quality, soil erosion and sedimentation, reduced groundwater resources, as well as reduced recreational and economic opportunities. These conditions engender the need to implement site-specific technologies and practices to filter and infiltrate stormwater and thereby reduce impacts from development.

This Ordinance encourages the use such technologies called Best Management Practices (BMPs) which are structural, vegetative, or managerial practices designed to treat, prevent, or reduce degradation of water quality due to stormwater runoff. All development projects subject to review under the requirements of this Ordinance shall be designed, constructed, and maintained using BMPs to prevent flooding, protect water quality, reduce soil erosion, maintain and contribute to the aesthetic values of the project. (Community) recognizes that PICP is one of several BMPs for achieving stormwater goals.

(b) General Requirements for PICP

    (1) The surfacing materials for pedestrian and vehicular uses shall consist of concrete paving units that conform to ASTM C936 including an average 8,000 psi compressive strength.

    (2) Whenever possible, PICP shall be used to reduce post-development peak flows and total water volumes to pre-development conditions. Pre-development is defined as the conditions on the existing site prior to the proposed development project.

    (3) Development plans shall be provided that include post-construction BMPs. PICP shall be designed to manage stormwater to help reduce local minor flooding, degradation of water quality related to stormwater runoff, and increase groundwater recharge and opportunities for water harvesting for irrigation where possible.

    (4) PICP shall be designed by a registered professional engineer or landscape architect and installed by a contractor who has successfully completed the requirements of the Interlocking Concrete Pavement Institute (ICPI) PICP Installer Technician Certificate course;

    (5) PICP shall include maintenance instructions to the property owner including a maintenance inspection schedule;

    (6) At a minimum, PICP surface, base/subbase shall be designed to adequately accommodate the rainfall depth of [insert local storm event requirements]. The base/subbase layers shall be designed to have sufficient detention capacity that stormwater will infiltrate into the soil below and can accommodate a second [insert local storm event requirements] depth within 5 days of the previous storm;

    (7) PICP shall be designed in accordance with guidelines in the ICPI manual, *Permeable Interlocking Concrete Pavements*, and guide specifications on www.icpi.org.

    (8) PICP shall be installed by a person holding an ICPI PICP Installer Technician Certificate who shall be onsite to oversee each installation crew during all PICP construction.

(c) Development of New Properties

    (1) Property is considered new property if the property proposed for development has no existing construction.

    (2) Impervious cover (total roof area, pedestrian and vehicular paving) shall not exceed a maximum of ___% of the total property according to the specific land use and zoning designation. See (reference section/pages) for specific land uses and maximum allowable impervious cover for each land use.

    (3) One-hundred (100) percent of the total area covered by PICP shall be considered a pervious or permeable surface.

(d) Re-development of Existing Properties

    (1) Property is considered existing property if the property proposed for re-development has existing construction.

    (2) Existing properties that do not exceed the maximum allowed impervious surface for new properties shall meet the requirements under (c) Development of New Properties.

    (3) Existing properties that exceed the maximum allowed impervious surface as stated in (c) Development of New Properties may construct new impervious surfaces if the proposed new impervious surface meets all setback and other regulations of this ordinance and if the following conditions are met:

        i. The applicant removes existing impervious surfaces exceeding the maximum allowed impervious surface under (c) Development of New Properties and restores those areas to a PICP surface at a 1 to 1 ratio.

        ii. Applicant shall submit a comprehensive stormwater management plan that emphasizes infiltration and onsite retention of stormwater for at the [insert design storm event(s)]. This shall be achieved through a combination of structural BMPs such as PICP and buffer strips, swales, rainwater gardens, bioswales, and other low impact development methods. The stormwater management plan must be designed by a registered professional engineer or landscape architect and installed as designed by a qualified contractor.

    (4) One-hundred (100) percent of the total area covered by PICP designed to allow for infiltration of water into the soil subgrade may be considered pervious;

    (5) A survey shall be submitted showing calculations of the exact dimensions of all existing impervious surfaces and of the lot before and after completion of the project;

    (6) In replacing existing impervious surfaces with surfaces designed to be PICP, the applicant must give priority to replacing those surfaces closest to natural bodies of water (lakes, ponds, rivers, streams or ocean) or those surfaces where the replacement is most likely to improve stormwater management;

(e) Streets and Access

    (1) PICP shall be considered a viable option for paving residential streets.

    (2) Street right-of-way widths shall be designed to reflect the minimum PICP required to accommodate the travel-way, parking lanes, sidewalks, and vegetated open channels.

    (3) PICP shall be considered a viable option for parking lanes on collector and thoroughfares.

(f) Parking Lots

    (1) Parking requirements shall be based on requirements described in (reference parking lot ordinance).

    (2) Parking lot designs shall reduce the overall impervious area by providing compact car spaces, minimizing stall dimensions, incorporating efficient parking lanes, and using PICP.

(g) Site Design

    (1) Direct rooftop runoff to PICP, open channels, or vegetated areas and avoid routing rooftop runoff to the roadway and to the stormwater conveyance system.

    (2) Create a variable width, naturally vegetated or permeable buffer system along all drainage ways that also encompasses critical environmental features such as the 100-year floodplain, steep slopes, and wetlands.

    (3) Minimize clearing and grading of woodlands and native vegetation to the minimum amount needed to build lots, allow access, and provide fire protection.

    (4) Conserve trees and other vegetation at each site by planting additional vegetation, clustering tree areas, and promoting the use of native plants.

    (5) Use PICP for paved areas and schedule installation to protect PICP from construction borne sediment.

    (6) Newly constructed stormwater outfalls to public waters must provide for filtering or settling of suspended solids and skimming of surface debris before discharge. PICP may be used as one method to achieve this requirement.

(h) Inspection and Maintenance Reporting

    (1) (Community) shall ensure that preventative maintenance is performed by inspecting PICP and all stormwater management systems draining into and from it.

    (2) Applicant shall provide an inspection plan and maintenance plan for PICP and other BMPs on the project site. Inspection reports shall be maintained by (community) for all stormwater management systems. Section(s) (___) provides inspection plans and maintenance requirements for other BMPs.

    (3) PICP inspection and maintenance shall include the items and intervals listed in the table below:

PICP Inspection and Maintenance Checklist	
Activity	**Frequency**
Vacuum/sweep surface	Annually, based on sediment loading. Power washing is not recommended.
Replenish aggregate in joints	As needed
Inspect vegetation and/or filter media around PICP perimeter for cover & soil stability	Annually, repair/replant as needed
Repair all surface deformations exceeding 1/2 in. (13 mm)	Annually, repair as needed
Repair pavers offset by more than 1/4 in. (6 mm) above/below adjacent units	Annually, repair as needed
Replace broken units impairing surface structural integrity	Annually, repair as needed
Check drainage inlets and outfalls for free flow of water & outflow and/or from observation well	Annually, after a major storm

References

AASHTO 1993. *Guide for Design of Pavement Structures*, American Association of State Highway and Transportation Officials, Washington, DC.

AASHTO 2004. *Guide for Mechanistic-Empirical Design of New And Rehabilitated Pavement Structures*, National Cooperative Highway Research Program, Transportation Research Board, National Research Council, American Association of State Highway and Transportation Officials, Washington, DC.

AASHTO 2010. "Geotextile Specification for Highway Applications," AASHTO Designation M-288, in Standard Specifications for Transportation Material and Methods of Sampling and Testing, Part IB: Specifications, 31st Edition, American Association for State Highway and Transportation Officials, Washington, DC.

ASCE 2010. *Structural Design of Interlocking Concrete Pavement for Municipal Streets and Roadways*, ASCE/T&DI/ICPI Standard 58-10, American Society of Civil Engineers, Reston, Virginia.

ASTM 2009. ASTM C 936, Standard Specification for Solid Concrete Interlocking Paving Units, *Annual Book of ASTM Standards*, Vol. 04.05, American Society for Testing and Materials International, Conshohocken, Pennsylvania.

ASTM 2009. ASTM C 1701 Standard Test Method for Infiltration Rate of In Place Pervious Concrete, *Annual Book of ASTM Standards*, Vol. 04.02, American Society for Testing and Materials International, Conshohocken, Pennsylvania.

ASTM 2011. ASTM E 1980 Standard Practice for Calculating Solar Reflectance Index of Horizontal and Low-Sloped Opaque Surfaces, *Annual Book of ASTM Standards*, Vol. 04.04, American Society for Testing and Materials International, Conshohocken, Pennsylvania.

Attarian 2010. Attarian, J. L., "Greener Alleys" in *Public Roads*, Vol. 73, No. 6, U.S. Federal Highway Administration, http://www.fhwa.dot.gov/publications/publicroads/10mayjun/05.cfm, Washington, DC.

Bäckström 2000. Bäckström, M., "Ground temperature in porous pavement during freezing and thawing," ASCE *Journal of Transportation Engineering*, Volume 126, Issue 5, pp. 375-381, American Society of Civil Engineers, September/October 2000.

Ballestero 2009. Ballestero, T. P., Roseen, R. M., Briggs, J. and Puls, T., "Reduction in Infiltration Capacity of Porous Asphalt and a Survey of Cleaning Methods and Their Effectiveness," presentation at Stormcon August 18, 2009, Anaheim, California, http://www.unh.edu/erg/cstev/Presentations/index.htm, University of New Hampshire Stormwater Center.

Bean 2005. Bean, E. Z., Hunt, W. F. and Bidelspach, D. A., "A Monitoring Field Study of Permeable Pavement Sites in North Carolina," in *Proceedings* of the 8th Biennial Conference on Stormwater Research & Watershed Management, Tampa, Florida, Southwest Florida Water Management District, April, 2005.

Bean 2007. Bean, E. Z., Hunt, W. F., and Bidelspach, D. A., "Field Survey of Permeable Pavement Surface Infiltration Rates," *Journal of Irrigation and Drainage Engineering*, May/June 2007, p. 249 – 255, American Society of Civil Engineers, Reston, Virginia.

Beecham 2009. Beecham, S., Pezzaniti, D., Myers, B., Shackel, B., and Pearson, A., "Experience in the Application of Permeable Interlocking Concrete Paving in Australia, " in *Proceedings* of the 9th International Conference on Concrete Block Paving, Buenos Aires, Argentina, Argentinean Concrete Block Association, Cordoba, Argentina, October 2009.

Beeldens 2006. "Environmental Friendly Concrete Pavement Blocks: Air Purification in the Centre of Antwerp," in *Proceedings* of the 8th International Conference on Concrete Block Paving, San Francisco, California, Interlocking Concrete Pavement Institute Foundation for Education and Research, Washington, DC.

Borgwardt 1994. Borgwardt, S., *Tests Performed on the Uni Eco-stone Pavements of Various Ages —Expert Opinion*, Institute for Planning Green Spaces and for Landscape Architecture, University of Hannover, Germany, July, 1994.

Borgwardt 1995. Borgwardt, S., "Suitable Beddings for Paving Blocks Permeable to Water," in *Betonwerk + Fertigteil-Technik* (Concrete Precasting Plant and Technology), March, 1995.

Borgwardt 1997. Borgwardt, S., "Performance and Fields of Application for Permeable Paving Systems," *Betonwerk + Fertigteil-Technik* (Concrete Precasting Plant and Technology), February, 1997, pp. 100 - 105.

Borgwardt 2006. "Long-Term In-Situ Infiltration Performance of Permeable Concrete Block Pavement," in *Proceedings* of the 8th International Conference on Concrete Block Paving, San Francisco, California, Interlocking Concrete Pavement Institute Foundation for Education and Research, Herndon, Virginia.

Brattebo 2003. Brattebo, B.O. and Booth D. B., "Long-Term Stormwater Quantity and Quality Performance of Permeable Pavement Systems," *Water Resources*, Vol. 37, pp. 4369-4376, Elsevier Press.

Cao 1998. Cao, S.L., Poduska, D. and Zollinger, D.G., *Drainage Design and Rutting Performance Guidelines for Permeable Pavement*, Texas A&M University, College Station, Texas, January 1998.

Caraco 1997. Caraco, D. and Claytor, R., *Stormwater BMP Design Supplement for Cold Climates*, Center for Watershed Protection, Ellicott City, Maryland, 1997.

Chopra 2007. Chopra. M., Waniliesta, M., Ballock, C., and Spence, J., *Construction and Maintenance Assessment of Pervious Concrete Pavements*, University of Central Florida, Orlando, Florida.

Chopra 2010. Chopra, M. B., Stuart, E. and Wanielista, M.P., "Pervious Pavement Systems in Florida – Research Results" in *Proceedings* of Low Impact Development 2010: Redefining Water in the City conference, San Francisco, California, American Society of Civil Engineers, Reston, Virginia.

Claytor 1996. Claytor, R.A., and Schueler T. R., *Design of Stormwater Filtering Systems*, Center for Watershed Protection, Ellicott City, Maryland, December 1996.

Clausen 2006. Clausen, J.C., and Gilbert, J. K., "Stormwater Runoff Quality and Quantity from Asphalt, Paver, and Crushed Stone Driveways in Connecticut," *Water Research*, Vol. 40, pp. 826-832, 2006.

Collins 2007. Collins, K.A., Hunt, W.F., Hathaway, J.M., *Hydrologic and Water Quality Comparison of Four Types of Permeable Pavement and Standard Asphalt In Eastern North Carolina*, Biological and Agricultural Engineering Department, North Carolina State University.

CSA 2006. Canadian Standards Association, A231.2-06, *Precast Concrete Pavers*, Rexdale, Ontario.

CWP 1998. *Better Site Design: A Handbook for Changing Development Rules in Your Community*, Center for Watershed Protection, Ellicott City, Maryland, August 1998.

Debo 1995. Debo, T. N. and Reese, A. J, *Municipal Storm Water Management*, Lewis Publishers, CBC Press, Boca Raton, Florida, 1995.

Dierks 2009. Dierks, S., *Hydrologic and Water Quality Performance Evaluation of Porous Pavers & Vegetated Swales on Easy Street in Ann Arbor, Michigan*, prepared for: Public Services Area, The City of Ann Arbor, Michigan, Stantec, Inc., November, 2009.

DOJ 2010. *ADA Standards for Accessible Design*, Department of Justice, Washington, DC, September 15, 2010.

Environment Canada 2010. *Canadian Climate Normals*, Atmospheric Environment Service, Environment Canada, http://climate.weatheroffice.gc.ca/Welcome_e.html, Toronto, Ontario, Canada.

Fairfax 1991. *Infiltration Design Considerations and Practices to Control Stormwater Runoff*, Handout from a Short Course, Fairfax County Department of Extension and Continuing Education, Fairfax County, Virginia, 1991.

FHWA 2002. *User's Guide for Drainage Requirements in Pavements – Drip 2.0 Microcomputer Program*, FHWA-IF-02-05C, Office of Pavement Technology, Federal Highway Administration

Gerrits 2002. Gerrits C. and James, W., "Restoration of Infiltration Capacity of Permeable Pavers," in *Proceedings* of the Ninth International Conference on Urban Storm Drainage, Portland, Oregon, American Society of Civil Engineers, Reston, Virginia, September, 2002.

Giroud 1988. Giroud, J. P., "Review of Geotextile Filter Criteria" in *Proceedings* of the 1st Indian Geotextiles Conference on Reinforced Soil and Geotextiles, Bombay, India, pp. 1–6.

Giroud 1996. Giroud, J. P., Granular Filters and Geotextile Filters. *Proceedings* of Geofilters '96, Montreal, Canada, pp. 565–680.

Hawkins 2009. Hawkins, R.H., Ward, T.J., Woodward, D.E. and Van Mullem, J.A., *Curve Number Hydrology —State of the Practice*, American Society of Civil Engineers, Reston, Virginia.

Hein 2006. Hein, D.K., "Resilient Modulus Testing of Open Graded Drainage Layer Aggregates for Interlocking Concrete Block Pavements," in *Proceedings* of the 8th International Conference on Concrete Block Paving, San Francisco, California, Interlocking Concrete Pavement Institute Foundation for Education & Research, November 2006.

Hershfield 1961. Hershfield, D.M., *Rainfall Frequency Atlas of the United States* (for durations from 30 minutes to 24 hours and return periods from 1 to 100 years), http://www.nws.noaa.gov/oh/hdsc/PF_documents/TechnicalPaper_No40.pdf , U.S. Department of Commerce, Weather Bureau, Technical Paper No. 40, Washington, DC.

Permeable Interlocking Concrete Pavements

Houle 2009. Houle, K.M., Roseen, R.M., Ballestero, T.P., Houle, J.J., "Performance Comparison of Porous Asphalt and Pervious Concrete Pavements in Northern Climates," Stormcon 2009, Forster Publications, Santa Monica, California.

ICPI 2006. *Tech Spec 8—Concrete Grid Pavements*, Interlocking Concrete Pavement Institute, Herndon, VA.

James 1997. James, W. and Thompson, M.K., "Contaminants from Four New Pervious and Impervious Pavements in a Parking-lot," in *Advances in Modeling the Management of Stormwater Impacts*, Vol. 5. W. James, Editor, Computational Hydraulics Inc., Guelph, Ontario, Canada, 1997, pages 207-222.

Jones 2010. Jones, D., Harvey, J., Li, T. and Campbell, B., *Laboratory Testing and Modeling for Structural Performance of Fully Permeable Pavements Under Heavy Traffic*, CTSW-RR-09-249.04D, California Department of Transportation Division of Environmental Analysis, Sacramento, California, April 2010.

Kevern 2009. Kevern, J.T., Schaefer, V.R. and Wang K., "Temperature Behavior of Pervious Concrete Systems," *Transportation Research Record: Journal of the Transportation Research Board No. 2098*, Transportation Research Board of the National Academies, Washington, DC, 2009, p. 94-101.

MIDS 2011. Table 7. Runoff and pollution reduction percentages, Minimal Impact Design Standards Work Group, Memo from Barr Engineering Company to MIDS Work Group, Minnesota Pollution Control Agency, St. Paul, Minnesota, February 11, 2010.

Miller 1973. Miller, J.F., Frederick, R.H. and Tracey R.J., *Precipitation-frequency Atlas of the Western United States*, Volumes I – XI, Atlas 2, http://www.nws.noaa.gov/oh/hdsc/noaaatlas2.htm , U.S. Department of Commerce, National Weather Service, National Ocean and Atmospheric Administration, Silver Spring, Maryland.

Newman 2002. Newman, A.P., Pratt, C.J., Coupe. S. J. and Cresswell, N., "Oil bio-degradation in Permeable Pavements by Microbial Communities," *Water Science and Technology*, Vol. 45, No 7, pp. 51–56. IWA Publishing.

NSA 1991. *The Aggregate Handbook*, National Stone Association, Washington, DC.

NVPDC 1999. Northern Virginia Planning District Commission, *Nonstructural Urban BMP Handbook*, Annandale, Virginia, December 1999.

Oram 2003. Oram, B., "Soils, Infiltration, and On-site Testing." Powerpoint presentation, www.bfenvironmental.com/presentations/soilsinfiltration.ppt, Wilkes University Geo-Environmental Sciences and Environmental Engineering Department, Wilkes-Barre, Pennsylvania.

PCA 2003. *Properties and Uses of Cement-Modified Soil*, Portland Cement Association, Skokie, Illinois, 2003.

Pitt 2002. Pitt, R., Chen, S. and Clark, S., "Compacted Urban Soils Effects on Infiltration and Bioretention Stormwater Control Designs," in *Proceedings* of the 9th International Conference on Urban Drainage, Portland, Oregon, September 8-13, 2002, American Society of Civil Engineers, Reston, Virginia.

Pratt 1999. Pratt, C. J., Newman, A. P. and Bond P.C., "Mineral Oil Biodegradation within a Permeable Pavement: Long Term Observations," *Water Science Technology*, Vol. 39, No. 2, pp. 103-109, Elsevier Science Ltd., Great Britain.

Raad 1994. Raad, L., Minassian, G.H. and Gartin, S., "Characterization of Saturated Granular Bases Under Repeated Loads," *Transportation Research Record: Journal of the Transportation Research Board*, No. 1369, Transportation Research Board of the National Academies, Washington, D.C., 1994, p. 73–82.

Reese 2007. Reese A.J., "Stormwater Utility User Fee Credits," in *Stormwater* magazine, November-December 2007, Forster Publications, Santa Monica, California.

Rollings 1992. Rollings, R.S. and Rollings M.P., *Applications for Concrete Paving Block in the United States Market*, Uni-Group U.S.A., http://www.uni-groupusa.org/manuals-lit.htm , Palm Beach Gardens, Florida.

Roseen 2009. Roseen, R.M., Ballestero, T.P., Houle, J.J., Avellaneda, P., Briggs, J., Fowler, G. and Wildey, R. "Seasonal Performance Variations for Storm-Water Management Systems in Cold Climate Conditions," *Journal of Environmental Engineering*, Vol. 135, No. 3, American Society of Civil Engineers, Reston, Virginia, March 2009.

Salem 2006. Salem, H., Bayomy, F., Smith, R. and Abdelrahman, M., "Effectiveness of Open-Graded Base Layer on Subgrade Moisture Regime and Overall Pavement Performance," *Transportation Research Record: Journal of the Transportation Research Board*, No. 1967, Transportation Research Board of the National Academies, Washington, D.C., 2006, p. 36–45.

Schwartz 2010. Schwartz, S.S., "Effective Curve Number and Hydrologic Design of Pervious Concrete Stormwater Systems," *Journal of Hydrologic Engineering*, Vol. 15, No. 6, American Society of Civil Engineers, Reston, Virginia. June 2010.

Shackel 2006. Shackel, B., "Design of Permeable Paving Subject to Traffic," in *Proceedings* of the 8th International Conference on Concrete Block Paving, San Francisco, California, Interlocking Concrete Pavement Institute Foundation for Education & Research, November 2006.

Shahin 1994. *The Leaching of Pollutants from Four Pavements Using Laboratory Apparatus*, Masters Thesis, University of Guelph, Guelph, Ontario, December 1994.

Stormcon 2010. Ballestero, T. P., Uribe, F., Roseen, R. and Houle, J., "The Porous Pavement Curve Number Conundrum," University of New Hampshire Stormwater Center, Durham, New Hampshire, Presentation at Stormcon 2010, San Antonio, Texas.

Swan 2009. Swan, D.J, and Smith, D.R., "Development of the Permeable Design Pro Permeable Interlocking Concrete Pavement Design System," in *Proceedings* of the 9th International Conference on Concrete Block Paving, Buenos Aires, Argentina, Argentinean Concrete Block Association, Cordoba, Argentina, October 2009.

Turf-Tec 2007. Turf-Tec Infiltrometer, http://www.turf-tec.com/IN2lit.html, Turf-Tec, Tallahassee, Florida.

Tyner 2009. Tyner, J.S., Wright, W.C., Dobbs, P.A., "Increasing exfiltration from pervious concrete and temperature monitoring," *Journal of Environmental Management*, 90 (2009) 2636–2641, Elsevier.

UNHSC 2008. *Porous Asphalt*, Fact Sheet issued by University of New Hampshire Stormwater Center, Durham, New Hampshire.

USDA 2003. Natural Resource Conservation Service, *NRCS National Engineering Handbook*, Part 630, Hyrdology, http://policy.nrcs.usda.gov/RollupViewer.aspx?hid=17092, Washington, DC.

USEPA 1997. *Urbanization and Streams: Studies of Hydrological Impacts*, U.S. Environmental Protection Agency, Office of Water (4503F), publication no. 841-R-97-009, http://water.epa.gov/polwaste/nps/urban/report.cfm#02, Washington, DC, December 1997.

USEPA 2005. *Stormwater Phase II Final Rule – An Overview*, U.S. Environmental Protection Agency, Office of Water, publication no. EPA 833-F-00-001, http://www.epa.gov/npdes/pubs/fact1-0.pdf, Washington, DC, December 2005.

USEPA 2008. *Green Parking Lot Resource Guide*, U.S. Environmental Protection Agency, Office of Solid Waste and Emergency Response, EPA-510-B-08-001, http://www.streamteamok.net/Doc_link/Green%20Parking%20Lot%20Guide%20(final).PDF, Washington, DC, February 2008.

USEPA. 2008. June 13 2008 Memo. L. Boornaizian and S. Heare. "Clarification on which stormwater infiltration practices/technologies have the potential to be regulated as "Class V" wells by the Underground Injection Control Program." Water Permits Division and Drinking Water Protection Division. Washington, D.C. Also see http://water.epa.gov/type/groundwater/uic/class5/index.cfm for additional information on Class V injection wells.

USEPA 2010. *Surface Infiltration Rates of Permeable Surfaces: Six Month Update* (November 2009 through April 2010), EPA/600/R-10/083, Office of Research and Development, National Risk Management Research Laboratory—Water Supply and Water Resources Division, Edison, New Jersey, June 2010.

USEPA 2010. "Permeable Interlocking Concrete Pavement Fact Sheet," http://cfpub.epa.gov/npdes/stormwater/menuofbmps/index.cfm?action=browse&Rbutton=detail&bmp=136&minmeasure=5, National Menu of Stormwater Best Management Practices, U.S. Environmental Protection Agency, Office of Water, Washington, DC.

USGBC 2009. *LEED Reference Guide for Green Building Design and Construction*, U.S. Green Building Council, Washington, DC.

VADCR 2010. Virginia DCR Stormwater Design Specification No. 7, Permeable Pavement, Version 1.7, Virginia Department of Conservation and Recreation, Richmond, Virginia.

Vancura 2010. Vancura, M., Khazanovich, McDonald, K., *Performance Evaluation of In-Service Pervious Concrete Pavements in Cold Weather*, Department of Civil Engineering, University of Minnesota, December 2010.

Van Seters 2007. Van Seters, T., *Performance Evaluation of Permeable Pavement and a Bioretention Swale Seneca College, King City, Ontario, Interim Report #3*, Toronto and Region Conservation Authority, Downsview, Ontario, May, 2007.

Yong 2008. Yong, C.F., Deletic, A., Fletcher, T.D., and Grace, M.R., "The Clogging Behaviour and Treatment Efficiency of a Range of Porous Pavements," in *Proceedings* of the 11th International Conference on Urban Drainage, Edinburgh, Scotland, United Kingdom, 2008.

Zement 2003. *Regenwasserversickerung durch Pflasterflachen*, Bauerberatung Zement, Zement-Merkblatt Strassenbau, Bundesverband der Deutsche Zementindustrie e.V., www.BDZement.de, Köln, Germany, S 15, June, 2003.

Appendix A—Glossary of Terms

AASHTO—American Association of State Highway and Transportation Officials

Aquifer—A porous water bearing geologic formation that yields water for consumption.

ASTM—American Society for Testing and Materials

Best Management Practice (BMP)—A structural or non-structural device designed to infiltrate, temporarily store, or treat stormwater runoff in order to reduce pollution and flooding.

Bioretention—A stormwater management practice that uses soils and vegetation to treat pollutants in urban runoff and to encourage infiltration of stormwater into the ground.

Bioretention basins—Landscaped depressions or shallow basins used to slow and treat on-site stormwater runoff. Stormwater is directed to the basin where it is treated by physical, chemical and biological processes. The slowed, cleaned water infiltrates native soils or is directed to nearby stormwater drains or receiving waters. PICP overflow can drain into such basins.

California Bearing Ratio or CBR—A test that renders an approximation (expressed as a percent) of the bearing strength of soil compared to that of a high quality, compacted aggregate base.

Cation—A positively charged atom or group of atoms in soil particles that, through exchange with ions of metals in stormwater runoff, enable those metals to attach themselves to soil particles.

Choke course—A layer of aggregate placed or compacted into the surface of another layer to provide stability and a smoother surface. The particle sizes of the choke course are generally smaller than those of the surface into which it is being pressed.

Clay soils—1. (Agronomy) Soils with particles less than 0.002 mm in size. 2. A soil textural class. 3. (Engineering) A fine-grained soil with more than 50% passing the No. 200 sieve with a high plasticity index in relation to its liquid limit, according the Unified Soil Classification System.

Combined sewer system or CSO—Conveyance of storm and sanitary sewage in the same pipes. CSOs are generally found in older urban areas. CSOs do significant damage to water quality resulting in diminished economic and recreational activities.

Crushed stone—Mechanically crushed rock that produces angular particles.

CSA—Canadian Standards Association

Curve Number (CN)—A numerical representation of a given area's hydrological soil group, plant cover, impervious cover, interception and surface storage. The U.S. Soil Conservation Service (SCS) originally developed the concept. A curve number is used to convert rainfall depth into runoff volume.

Dense-graded base—Generally a crushed aggregate base with fines that, when compacted, creates a foundation for pavements and does not allow significant amounts of water into it. Particle sizes can range from 1.5 in. (40 mm) to smaller than the No. 200 (0.075 mm) sieve.

Detention pond or structure—The temporary storage of stormwater runoff in an area with objective of decreasing peak discharge rates and providing a settling basin for pollutants.

Equivalent Single Axle Loads or ESALs—Characterization of all axle loads that render damage to pavements and used as a means to define pavement life; one ESAL is 18,000 lbs or 80 kN.

Erosion—The process of wearing away of soil by water, wind, ice, and gravity. 2. Detachment and movement of soil particles by same.

Evapotranspiration—The return of moisture to the atmosphere from the evaporation of water from soil and transpiration from vegetation.

Exfiltration—The downward movement of water through an open-graded, crushed stone base into the soil beneath.

Fines—Silt and clay particles in a soil, generally those smaller than the No. 200 or 0.075 mm sieve.

First flush—The initial portion of a rainstorm that flushes high concentrations of accumulated

pollutants into the storm drainage system. High concentrations are usually due to antecedent dry weather conditions that create an accumulation of pollutants on pavements washed away by the rainstorm.

Grade—1. (Noun) The slope or finished surface of an excavated area, base, or pavement usually expressed in percent. 2. (Verb) To finish the surface of same by hand or with mechanized equipment.

Gravel—1. Aggregate ranging in size from 1/4 in. (6 mm) to 3 in. (75 mm) which naturally occurs in streambeds or riverbanks that has been smoothed by the action of water. 2. A type of soil as defined by the Unified Soil Classification System having particle sizes ranging from the No. 4 sieve (4.75 mm) and larger.

Hotspot—A land use that generates highly contaminated runoff with concentrations higher than those typical to stormwater.

Hydrological Soil Group—The soils classification system developed by the U.S. Soil Conservation Service (now the Natural Resource Conservation Service) that categorizes soils into four groups, A through D, based on runoff potential. A soils have high permeability and low runoff whereas D soils have low permeability and high runoff.

Impervious cover—Any surface in the built environment that prohibits percolation and infiltration of rainwater into the ground; a term for pavements and roofs.

Infiltration rate—The rate at which stormwater moves through soil measured in inches per hour or meters per second.

Interlocking concrete pavement—A system of paving consisting of discrete, hand-sized paving units with either rectangular or dentated shapes manufactured from concrete. Either type of shape is placed in an interlocking pattern, compacted into coarse bedding sand, the joints filled with sand and compacted again to start interlock. The paving units and bedding sand are placed over an unbound or bound aggregate layer. Also called concrete block pavement.

Karst geology—Regions of the earth underlain by carbonate rock typically with sinkholes and/or limestone caverns.

MS4s—Municipal Separate Storm Sewer System: A conveyance or system of conveyances that is:
- Owned by a state, city, town, village, or other public entity that discharges to waters of the U.S.;
- Designed or used to collect or convey stormwater (including storm drains, pipes, ditches, etc.);
- Not a combined sewer; and
- Not part of a Publicly Owned Treatment Works (sewage treatment plant)

Observation well—A perforated pipe inserted vertically into an open-graded base used to monitor its infiltration rate.

One year storm—A rainfall event that has a 100% chance of occurring in a given year.

One hundred year storm—A very unusual rainfall event that has a 1% chance of occurring in a given year.

Open-graded base—Generally a crushed stone aggregate material used as a pavement base that has no fine particles in it. The void spaces between aggregate can store water and allow it to freely drain from the base.

Outlet—The point at which water is discharged from an open-graded base through pipes into a stream, lake, river, or storm sewer.

Peak discharge rate—The maximum instantaneous flow from a detention or retention pond, open-graded base, pavement surface, storm sewer, stream or river usually related to a specific storm event.

Permeability—The rate of water movement through a soil column under saturated conditions, usually expressed as k in calculations per specific ASTM or AASHTO tests, and typically expressed in inches per hour or meters per second.

Permeable interlocking concrete pavement—Concrete pavers with wide joints (5 mm to 10 mm) or a pattern that creates openings in which rainfall and runoff can infiltrate. The joints/openings are filled with permeable aggregate. The pavers and a permeable aggregate bedding layer are typically placed on an open-graded aggregate base/subbase which filters, stores, infiltrates, and/or drains runoff. Sand is not used within the pavement structure.

Permeable pavement—A surface with penetrations capable of passing and spreading water capable of supporting pedestrians and vehicles, e.g. permeable interlocking concrete pavement.

Pervious or permeable surfaces/cover— Surfaces that allow the infiltration of rainfall such as vegetated areas.

Porosity—Volume of voids in a base divided by the total volume of a base.

Porous pavement—A surface full of pores capable of supporting pedestrians and vehicles, e.g. porous asphalt, porous concrete (cast-in-place or precast units).

Pretreatment—BMPs that provide storage and filtering pollutants before they enter another BMP for additional filtering, settling, and/or processing of stormwater pollutants.

Rain gardens—Gardens containing flowers and grasses (preferably native species of both) that can survive in soil soaked with water from rain storms. Rain gardens do not have standing water. Rain gardens collect and slow stormwater run off and increase infiltration into the soil.

Retention pond—A body of water that collects runoff and stays full permanently. Runoff flowing into the pond that exceeds its capacity is released into a storm sewer, stream, lake, or river.

Runoff coefficient—Ratio of surface runoff to rainfall expressed a number from 0 to 1.

Sand—1. (Agronomy) A soil particle between 0.05 and 2.0 mm in size. 2. A soil textural class. 3. (Engineering) A soil larger than the No. 200 (0.075 mm) sieve and passing the No.4 (4.75 mm) sieve, according to the Unified Soil Classification System (USCS).

Sediment—Soils transported and deposited by water, wind, ice, or gravity.

Sheet flow—The laminar movement of runoff across the surface of the landscape.

Silt—1. (Agronomy) A soil consisting of particles sizes between 0.05 and 0.002 mm. 2. A soil textural class. 3. (Engineering) A soil with no more than 50% passing the No. 200 (0.075 sieve) that has a low plasticity index in relation to the liquid limit, according to the Unified Soil Classification System.

Structural Number (SN)—A calculation used by AASHTO to assesses the structural capacity of a pavement handle loads based on ESALs and soil subgrade strength.

Swale—A small linear topographic depression that conveys runoff

Time of concentration—The time runoff takes to flow to a drainage area's most distant point to the point of drainage such as storm sewer inlet.

TMDL—Total Maximum Daily Load - A term in the U.S. Clean Water Act describing the maximum amount of a pollutant a body of water can receive without significantly impairing the water quality or health of the existing aquatic ecosystem.

Void Ratio—Volume of voids around the aggregate divided by the volume of solids.

About the Author

David R. Smith is the Technical Director for the Interlocking Concrete Pavement Institute ICPI (www.icpi.org). Key players in the industry and he started the ICPI in 1993 with 66 charter members. At this writing, the association has over 1000 members representing producers, contractors and suppliers.

Since 1987, he has worked with architects, engineers, landscape architects and contractors on design and construction of every kind of concrete paver project from patios to streets, to ports and airports. Besides publishing dozens of articles, peer reviewed technical papers, guide specifications and ICPI Tech Spec technical bulletins on interlocking concrete, permeable, slab and grid pavements, Mr. Smith has written much of three ICPI student and instructor manuals for segmental concrete pavement contractors and taught many classes. Also, he authored three design idea books for residential, commercial and municipal applications. He has also contributed to ICPI engineering design manuals for port and airport pavements constructed with interlocking concrete pavements.

As a leading authority in North America on concrete segmental paving and permeable paving, Mr. Smith regularly speaks at national and international conferences. He is a past chair of CSA A231 on precast concrete paving products. He is active in ASTM, having written and revised several ASTM standards and test methods on concrete paving products. He is a member of the ASCE Permeable Pavements Technical Committee and editor since 1994 of the quarterly *Interlocking Concrete Pavement Magazine* (circ. 25,000) which features stories on interlocking and permeable interlocking concrete pavement.

In the early and mid-1980s, Mr. Smith studied European approaches to urban climatology, green infrastructure, neighborhood design and traffic calming. He served on a UNESCO Man and Biosphere committee that studied urban climatology, the urban heat island and the benefits of urban forestry and green infrastructure for reducing runoff, air pollution and summer electrical consumption in U.S. cities. He has contributed to national and international conferences on urban forestry and green infrastructure management. In 1987, he consulted with the City of Valencia, Spain on the urban climate benefits of that city's master plans to plant street trees, revitalize parks and expand green space.

His background in stormwater management comes from infiltration research on concrete grid pavements in the early 1980s at Virginia Tech, as well as teaching and modeling storm drainage design with sustainable, site-scale stormwater management approaches and stream restoration. More recently, Mr. Smith contributed to the concept and development of ICPI's *Permeable Design Pro* software for PICP.

Mr. Smith was editor of and contributor to the 2006 *Proceedings* of the 8th International Conference on Concrete Block Paving held in San Francisco, California, which was hosted by the ICPI Foundation for Education and Research. Mr. Smith is Secretary-Treasurer of the Small Element Pavement Technologists (www.sept.org), segmental paving experts from around the world whose mission is to perpetuate the triennial international conferences on interlocking concrete pavement and related segmental concrete pavement systems. The group also maintains a database of technical papers from the international conferences dating back to their start in 1980. His education includes a bachelor of Architecture and masters of Urban and Regional Planning with a concentration in environmental planning from Virginia Tech.

There are also "double houses", square ones usually (but with notable exceptions) with four rooms to a floor, some of them from the Georgian period, many influenced by the Adam style. As Mr. Stoney has said, the double house has its own peculiarities. "To get room for really sumptuous parlors it puts them upstairs where they can run over the space occupied below by a central hall, and where also their coved ceilings can be carried up into the roof space. As a rule the Double House is in every way more pretentious in its decorations than the Single House . . ."

The earliest of the city's houses, reflecting the simple tastes—and more limited incomes—of the first generations gave way to more sophisticated

90-92-94 Church Street. (Right to left) Fine examples of the Charleston "single house". The sidewalk door is in reality a formal entrance to the piazza; the actual front door is secluded from the street. These three houses date from 1730 to 1805.

Governor Joseph Alston and his wife, Theodosia Burr, lived at No. 94.

ones after 1720, the year the British Crown assumed control of the colony. By 1750, Charleston was known as "the richest and most eminent city in the southern part of North America . . . 1500 houses, regular streets and many fine buildings."

In an era of prosperity unbroken until the Revolution, Charlestonians built in the grand manner—St. Michael's Church, and mansions like those of Miles Brewton and Colonel John Stuart. After the Revolution, in an even greater tide of prosperity that followed a depression, the city's builders embraced the Adam style. From this period date the remarkable spiral stairs and oval, as well as octagonal, rooms, delicately decorated mantels and cornices.

Charleston's most celebrated architects worked after the Revolution. One of the most talented and best known was an "amateur" of independent means who produced designs for his family and friends. Gabriel Manigault was a descendant of an early Huguenot refugee; his earliest known house design is the Joseph Manigault House, which was built for his brother. His other work includes the South Carolina Society Hall and the City Hall.

Robert Mills, another native Charlestonian, was the first of the trained, professional architects known to have worked in the city. To him are attributed

100 Meeting Street. Fireproof Building. Completed in 1828, this structure was the work of architect Robert Mills, who used brick, stone and iron in what was the first attempt in this country to erect a completely fireproof building. It once was the County Records Building. Recently restored, it is occupied by the South Carolina Historical Society.

Intricate details of window cornices form interesting shadow patterns and also break direct sun rays on these Broad Street offices.

the Fireproof Building, the Marine Hospital and the First Baptist Church. (Mills was well known nationally and was the architect for the Washington Monument in the District of Columbia as well as buildings in Philadelphia, Baltimore, Richmond, Columbia, Mobile and New Orleans.)

E. B. White possibly was Charleston's most prolific architect. A number of his best buildings date to the 1840's. He designed, among others, the present Huguenot Church, Grace Church, Market Hall, the portico and wings of the College of Charleston and the St. Philip's Church steeple.

And to collaborate with architects and builders were iron workers in remarkable number, cabinetmakers who produced "Charleston pieces" by the score, wood carvers and highly skilled plasterers who fashioned the medallions and cornices to decorate the grand drawing rooms.

Along with the rich historical and architectural heritage, the modern city's social life has roots in the past. To an outsider, these ties seem remarkably close but if they are, it is understandable—a number of benevolent and welfare societies founded before 1750 are still active.

Among them is the St. Andrew's Society, which was organized in 1729 by residents of Scot descent "to assist all people in distress." Before the Revolution, civic-conscious residents had founded the Charleston Library Society, the Charleston Museum (the nation's oldest city museum), and the St. Cecelia Society. The latter, begun as a music group in 1762, first devoted itself to dancing in 1822 when there was a shortage of musicians. The St. Cecilia Ball is now held each year in January, a brilliant social occasion on the local calendar.

In the section of the country long noted for its hospitality, it may well be that Charleston made that reputation for the South. Entertaining guests, and being entertained, is an enjoyment long practiced by residents. For many years, Race Week was Charleston's most important and festive event. Shops closed and business came to a standstill when the fine blooded horses were brought to race for fame—and sometimes for small fortunes.

Diaries and letters from all but the most tragic times recount dinners, balls, parties of all descriptions—with the elegant and distinctive cuisine always an important part of the festivities. Fine cellars were kept by all who could afford them. Madeira was the favorite wine, and, from all accounts, it was consumed in quantity with other spirits; one visitor exclaimed that nowhere else had he been served such rich wines.

Along with the wine and spirits, there is a cuisine that is particularly Charleston in both ingredients and preparation. (For those who would try their talents in preparing Charleston dishes, *Charleston Receipts* is an admirable source of instruction.) Epicures admire many of the dishes, but have extra plaudits for "She-Crab Soup".

The essence of Charleston's charm is not in architecture and customs alone. A touring Rhode Islander, Elkanah Watson, noted after the Revolution that the place had an "almost Asiatic splendor." One modern scholar has called it "the sensuous city", whose natural beauties have endured through the generations—a place with sights, sounds, tastes, and aromas all its own. It is washed by the smells of rivers and marshes and sea mists. It is noteworthy, perhaps, that even the smallest gardens usually have aromatic flowering shrubs.

Solid window shutters keep out harsh sunlight and provide privacy to houses that abut the sidewalks. These were photographed on Church Street.

21 Cumberland Street. Old Powder Magazine. The only public building known to have survived from the days of the Lords Proprietors, this sturdy structure stood inside the walls that originally encompassed the city. Designed to store powder, the walls are two feet eight inches thick and are capped by a groined vaulting of brick and oyster shell mortar.

The basic construction is of "tabby", an early building material made by burning oyster shells to obtain lime, then mixed with shells to form an excellent and durable concrete.

The magazine is owned and operated as a museum by the National Society of the Colonial Dames of America in The State of South Carolina.

There is an almost endless breath of fragrance from gardens—wintersweet and jasmine, daphne and banana shrub, tea olive and pittosporum, sweet bay and magnolia, loquat and wisteria, jessamine and honeysuckle.

The blend of enticing sounds was little changed before the age of the automobile—endless calls of shore and song birds, ships in harbor, lapping water, pounding surf, the musical accents of Negro voices (in early days contrasting with a Babel of English, French, Portuguese, Dutch, Spanish and the burrs of Scots merchants and gutturals of Cherokee Chiefs).

To be sure, it was never all beauty and sweet scents. A seaport, busy and

Graceful wrought iron affords a sense of privacy, but does not block the view of passersby into this garden on lower Church Street.

prosperous, has, by its very nature, a bitter side. Charleston has had her share; a devoted community is trying, and with success, to clear away the scars of neglect and preserve its abundant beauty.

Many a visitor to Charleston carries away a vision of mellowing houses and narrow streets set amid a vast garden of tropical luxuriance, walled, fenced and hedged, but barely contained.

The gardening tradition is almost as old as the first settlement.

In 1682, two years after the city was moved to the present site, one Thomas Ash recorded that: "Gardens begin to be supplied with such European plants and Herbs as are necessary for the Kitchen . . . Gardens also begin to be beautiful and adorned with such Herbs and Flowers which to the Smell or Eye are pleasing and agreeable, viz. the Rose, Tulip, Carnation and Lilly, etc."

No American city has a richer horticultural tradition. Numerous talented botanists and landscape architects of the 17th and 18th centuries came here to work, drawn by the rich variety of the native flora.

The first gardeners transplanted trees and shrubs of the countryside—live oaks, magnolias, bays, palmettoes, wild fruits, hollies, dogwood, redbud, shadbush, silverbell, deciduous azaleas, yuccas, witch hazel, fringe trees, sweet pepperbush, button bush, red buckeye. Luxuriant vines from the woodlands soon scrambled over garden walls—yellow jessamine, coral honeysuckle, trumpet creeper, crossvine, and the pale blue clematis known locally as "Travelling Joy".

By 1710 the English historian John Lawson was describing these wonders to his countrymen back home, and he was followed by Mark Catesby, "the Colonial Audubon", a self-trained artist sent out by Sir Hans Sloane, founder of the British Museum.

Catesby introduced to England many Carolina exotics, including the magnolia, whose foot-wide blooms opened on a Devonshire estate as early as 1735, to the delight of its owner, Sir John Colleton: "Its ample and fragrant blossoms, the curious structure of its purple cones and pendant scarlet seeds, successively adorn and perfume the woods from May to October." From Charleston, Catesby did much of the exploration that

resulted in his masterpiece, *The Natural History of Carolina, Florida and the Bahama Islands.*

There were also the father-and-son botanists from Philadelphia, John and William Bartram. John corresponded and exchanged plants and seeds with Charleston gardeners, and William set out from the city on his exploration of the Deep South in 1773 of which he wrote his celebrated *Travels Through North and South Carolina.*

Most famous of Charleston's early botanists was André Michaux, who arrived in 1786 to collect specimens for the French government. He bought a tract of some 100 acres outside the city as a nursery, and shipped home more than 6000 plants—few of which survived. He also imported plants that were to become so familiar that the South adopted them as its own: crepe myrtle, mimosa, chinaberry and the fragrant tea olive. By tradition it was also Michaux who introduced *Camellia japonica* and the Indian azaleas, which have become the chief ingredients of beauty in the Low Country garden landscapes.

An amateur Charleston botanist, Dr. Alexander Garden, who introduced many native plants to cultivation, became so expert that his correspondent, the great Swedish taxonomist Linnaeus, named the fragrant Chinese native, the *Gardenia,* in his honor.

Many others helped to form the city's gardening traditions: Dr. Thomas Dale, who arrived in 1725; Dr. Thomas Walter, who planted one of the first American botanical gardens outside the city and wrote the most complete 18th century work of its kind, *Flora Caroliniana . . .,* a book that described about 1000 species (Governor John Drayton, himself an amateur botanist, translated Walter's work from the Latin); Joel R. Poinsett, who introduced from Mexico the vividly-colored plant known as *Poinsettia.*

Charleston's private gardens developed rapidly through these generations of horticultural activity. By 1734 a landscape architect from London, Peter Chassereau, was laying out "grounds for Gardens or Parks in a grand and rural manner" and a successor soon offered his services for building fountains, waterworks, grottoes and vineyards. Even earlier, in 1732, "the best garden seeds" had been offered for sale in *The South Carolina Gazette.* Importers also sold a variety of bulbs and

31 Meeting Street. Several water fountains, similar to this one, add to a feeling of repose.

roots: tulips, anemones, narcissus, tuberoses, hyacinths, poppies, carnations and roses.

Local nurserymen served several gardeners of the city and nearby plantations. In 1745 Richard Lake's Ashley River nursery offered "Lemon Trees with Lemons on them in Boxes, Lime Trees and Orange Trees." Twenty years later activity had become so brisk that John Watson, a British gardener for Henry Laurens, sold not only seeds, plants and roots, but also "spades, rakes, reels, lines, watering pots, scythes, furniture and rub-stones, garden and Dutch hoes, watering engines, budding and pruning knives."

The merchant Laurens and his wife, enthusiastic gardeners, imported plants from many parts of the world: olives, capers, limes, ginger, the Alpine strawberry, raspberries, blue grapes, fine French apples, plums and pears.

The earliest Charleston examples have gone the way of most ancient gardens, but though plantings and walkways and even walls disappeared without leaving traces, many accurate garden drawings have been preserved. Many are to be seen in the Charleston Museum and several have been published. Largely due to the skill, devotion, scholarship and unwavering determination of Miss Emma Richardson, many of today's gardens are accurate reflections of their predecessors in design, horticultural material and in spirit.

Though the formal designs of most Charleston gardens reflect their English and European (particularly French) heritage, with their box-bordered paths, geometrically proportioned beds, brick walls and iron gates, the adaptations are Charleston's own. In the luxuriance of their growth through the long, slow seasons, their endless variety of form, color, texture and fragrance, the gardens of the old city are distinctive; a visitor is tempted to say unique.

Charleston's international fame as a garden center was largely won by the incomparable landscapes of great plantation gardens outside the city—in particular, Middleton Place, Magnolia and Cypress Gardens. These three attractions alone have drawn millions of visitors from many parts of the world.

Middleton Place, with its butterfly lakes, great drifts of azaleas and allées of camellias, is the oldest landscaped garden in the country. When the invading Federal troops swept through the area, the plantation house was burned and the Middleton family could no longer maintain the property. After years of neglect, Middleton Place has once more become one of the great gardens of the world.

Magnolia Gardens, situated near Middleton Place, was originally

Live oaks, usually festooned with Spanish moss, thrive in the semi-tropical Charleston climate. This beauty hugs the shore of the Ashley River, on the grounds of Magnolia Gardens.

named for a magnificent row of magnolia trees stretching to the river. Pre-World War I Baedekers for the United States listed three two-star items for travellers: the Grand Canyon, Niagara Falls and Magnolia Gardens.

Cypress Gardens was planted more recently; in the 18th century, the lake was a "reserve" used for flooding the fields by a rice planter. Masses of azaleas and flowering spring bulbs are reflected in the inky, still waters; overhead, the great cypress trees sift the sunlight.

Middleton Place and Magnolia Gardens are on the Ashley River, Cypress Gardens on the Cooper River. To professional and amateur botanists, and to lovers of beauty, all three come close to being shrines.

Preservation of Charleston's historic houses and buildings is successful and continuing. A great deal remains to be done, but it requires time, money and effort. Archaeological studies are in progress on several sites, and planning for future projects is the concern of both individuals and organizations.

This great effort is being made not only for Charleston and her residents, but for all Americans.

87 Church Street. Heyward-Washington House. The three-story brick house in the center of the picture was built by a wealthy rice planter, Daniel Heyward. The interior, finished in fine cypress paneling, houses a notable collection of Charleston furniture.

George Washington was a guest here on his official Southern tour in 1791.

Before restoration, this historic house had been defaced by a baker who installed a plate glass window; the kitchen had been used as a pool hall. Now owned by the Charleston Museum, the main house, kitchen and garden are open to the public. Admission fee.

On the right (89-91 Church Street) is Catfish Row, of Dubose Heyward's *Porgy*.

*". . . the most
civilized town
in the world."*

38-40-44 Tradd Street. (right to left)
Almost all the dwellings in this block
date to colonial times; they barely
escaped the disastrous fire of 1778 that
destroyed many of the pre-
Revolutionary buildings. Two of the
earliest in this group date to 1718. The
street may have been named for the first
male child born in the young city.

Gardens in the rear of the Heyward-Washington House are laid out in typical eighteenth century style. Perhaps because of their memories of English gardens, colonists liked and used the formal, stylized use of boxwood. This garden was designed by Miss Emma Richardson. It is maintained by the Garden Club of Charleston.

One of the finest pieces of furniture ever made in America, the secretary-bookcase in the Heyward-Washington House combines Chippendale and Hepplewhite styles. It was made locally, although the cabinetmaker responsible is not known. The books on its shelves were gathered from local private libraries; many of them bear the 18th century bookplates of John Bee Holmes, an early owner of the bookcase. This piece is known as the "Holmes breakfront".

The mahogany breakfast table, and also the chairs, date from 1760 to 1790 and are attributed to Thomas Elfe.

Thomas Elfe, one of the most prolific and talented Charleston cabinetmakers, produced fretwork like this over a mantel of the Heyward-Washington House. Several other similar pieces are attributed to Elfe.

51 Meeting Street. Nathaniel Russell House. The prosperous merchant, who came from Rhode Island to Charleston before the Revolution, had completed this house by 1809. The main structure is of Carolina gray brick trimmed with red brick. Russell's initials can

be seen in the cartouche of the front panel of the wrought iron balcony which is continuous and extends across the front and side of the house.

This imposing home, built at the enormous cost of $80,000, boasts oval, square and rectangular rooms, and Adam style mantels, overdoors and overwindows. The furnishings are of the period.

Historic Charleston Foundation acquired the house in 1955 and has its headquarters here. Open to the public year around with an admission fee.

A dramatic view of the free-flying spiral stairway of the Nathaniel Russell House, one of the architectural gems of the city. This striking photograph was taken from the third floor.

Steeple, St. Michael's Church. The clock and eight bells in this steeple were installed in 1764. The clock is the "official" timepiece for the city. Although the church building survived the 1886 earthquake, the 186-foot-high steeple sank eight inches from the tremor.

80 Broad Street. City Hall, seen through a window of St. Michael's Church. Designed by Gabriel Manigault, Charleston's "gentleman architect", in 1801, this building was acquired by the city in 1818. Of special interest are the bull's eye grills and the two rear basement window grills, of wrought iron.

St. Michael's is the oldest church building in the city, although not the oldest parish. Its cornerstone was laid in 1752 and the first services were held in 1761. Samuel Cardy is thought to have been the architect.

The "defects" in the two St. Michael's window panes are marks left by the glassblower's pipe.

21 East Battery. Edmondston-Alston House. Now open to the public as a house museum of Historic Charleston Foundation, this elegant town house was built about 1828 by Charles Edmondston. Charles Alston, a Georgetown County rice planter, purchased the house ten years later.

The house, with elaborate and unconventional woodwork, also contains a fine collection of Alston family furnishings.

Books in the Edmondston-Alston library have not left the residence since they were acquired; most of them are now collectors' items. The furniture here, like that in the rest of the house, is part of the Alston family collection.

83-108 East Bay. Rainbow Row. An arched passage frames a magnificent wrought iron gate in this colorful row of buildings. When eighteenth century merchants built here, gateways led to gardens, from which private stairways rose to the second

story living quarters. There was no access from the first floor shop directly to the second floor.

The buildings are derivative of both English and Dutch architecture and were erected between 1720 and 1787. In Colonial times, they fronted directly on the water, giving the merchants quick and easy access to nearby ships.

99-101 East Bay. This is an interior of the first of the row houses to be restored on what is now known as "Rainbow Row". The restoration took place in 1932 after the entire block had deteriorated into slums.

The private dwelling contains a number of Charleston-made pieces, some of them shown here. The library walls, paneled in cypress, were stripped of many coats of paint during the restoration.

The Sword Gates, at 32 Legare Street. This famous iron work was done by Christopher Werner in the nineteenth century, who originally designed the gates for the city.

94 Rutledge Avenue. Mikell House. A prosperous Edisto Island cotton planter, Isaac Jenkins Mikell, built this 1853 house as a wedding present for his third bride. Used as a winter residence until the War Between the States, the building is one of the finest examples of Greek Revival architecture in the city. The extensive gardens have been restored to the period of the house.

Ram's head capitals atop the six composite columns of the Mikell House.

27 King Street. Miles Brewton House. Completed in 1769, this has been called "perhaps the finest Colonial town house in America". Certainly, it is one of the finest Georgian houses ever erected in this country. Miles Brewton was both wealthy and influential; he was a member of the Commons House of Assembly for many years.

The British commander, Gen. Sir Henry Clinton, lived here when the city was occupied during the Revolution, and the Union Generals Hatch and Meade made it headquarters during the War Between the States.

The house and courtyard dependencies, remaining unaltered, present an accurate 18th century picture.

Admired in the 18th century as one of the truly beautiful and perfect rooms in the country, the Miles Brewton drawing room has lost none of its charm through the centuries. The Irish crystal chandelier, still lit by candles, dominates the large room that stretches almost the entire width of the second floor front of the mansion.

Detail of the carved woodwork which is found throughout the Miles Brewton house. Such magnificent work helps explain why the house took ten years to build.

A rear view of the Miles Brewton house, showing (on the left) the 18th century servants' quarters and kitchens, and a corner of the formal garden. The garden, whose striking box-bordered beds are of 18th century design, is part of the larger original which once extended to the water.

64 South Battery. William Gibbes House. The marble stairway on the front facade was added to this 1772 house in 1800. Considered of national importance, this large home is a fine example of Georgian architecture. The second floor drawing room is regarded as one of the most beautiful rooms in the country.

17 Chalmers Street. The Pink House. This appealing small building, one of the most-photographed of Charleston originals, is believed to have been a tavern in the Colonial period. The tile roof is characteristic of early Charleston.

The East Battery at high tide. For almost three centuries Charlestonians labored to reclaim the marshy waterfront along the Cooper River, filling with stones and other heavy material after each major storm. Finally, this masonry barrier was completed, holding back the raging waters that gale winds often fling at the city's vulnerable perimeter.

7-9 Stoll's Alley. Justinius Stoll built No. 7 (in the foreground) in the mid-18th century and this charming narrow passageway bears his name. The adjoining house is also pre-Revolutionary.

Corner, East Battery and South Battery. An Oleander (Nerium oleander) in full bloom. The plant was first introduced into England from Southern Europe in 1596, and brought to Charleston by the city's early gardeners, perhaps before the end of the seventeenth century. Very much at home in Charleston's climate, the oleander blooms throughout most of the summer.

106 Broad Street. Lining House. Dr. John Lining's house narrowly escaped the great fire of 1861. The oldest wooden building in the city, it was used as an apothecary shop from 1780 until 1962, when it was restored by the Preservation Society of Charleston.

Dr. Lining made the first scientific weather observations in the country.

110 Broad Street. Harvey House. Constructed prior to 1728 by William Harvey, this twelve-room house has been called an "architectural museum piece." It has remained virtually unchanged, and in the same family, since it was built.

Much of the floor-to-ceiling paneling is very wide; there are three-foot-wide planks over several mantels. There are also many unusual building features: six-foot-wide hinged doors, chimneys that provide their usual function but also act as beam supports, door frames set into arched openings.

172 Rutledge Avenue. Ashley Hall. Built as a residence by Patrick Duncan about 1815 and occupied for several years by George A. Trenholm, treasurer of the Confederate States, Ashley Hall has been in use as a private girls' school since 1909.

The interior is distinguished by a spiral staircase soaring from the ground floor to the roof, and by magnificent carved woodwork and paneling. The ground floor piazza, originally open, was enclosed in comparatively recent years.

631 East Bay Street. Faber House. This 1839 Palladian mansion, suffering from damage and neglect that began during the city's occupation by Union forces in 1865, was saved by the Historic Charleston Foundation. Now restored, it houses business offices. The hexagonal cupola still provides a vantage spot to view the harbor; in early days, tidal creeks flowed by the portico.

42 Society Street. The perfectly scaled furnishings of this dining room include an English tazza and claret jugs of about 1800 on an octagonal English table dating from the first half of the 18th century. The barometer, also English, was made by Robert Masefield in 1767. The portrait is an early 19th century likeness of Arthur Middleton of Stono.

64 Meeting Street. A small town garden at the peak of azalea season, with hyacinths and tulips also in bloom. The handsome tree on the left is a crepe myrtle, often unfamiliar to visitors to the South. The residence is a typical single house with a secluded piazza.

21 King Street. Patrick O'Donnell House. This typically Charleston tier of soaring piazzas is attached to an Italian Renaissance style residence. Built by an Irish master mason, the main house was completed about 1856. Of special note are the facade's decorative details. Unusually well constructed, the central portion survived the 1886 earthquake. The older library wing suffered such damage that it had to be rebuilt in 1887.

The Exchange Building. Although it has not been as well publicized as the Boston Tea Party, Charles Town had its protest against the tax on tea which had been levied by the British Parliament. The protest meeting was held in the Great Hall of the Exchange Building on Dec. 3, 1773, following the arrival in port of a consignment of 257 chests of tea on board the *London*. At the meeting, three consignees of the cargo were asked to agree not to accept the shipment; they agreed. Later, a second meeting was held and a resolution passed that no tea would be "landed, received or vended" until the taxation on tea was repealed.

Charleston's most historic building was then sparkling new. Begun in 1767, it had been completed in 1771 by Peter and John Horlbeck on plans drawn by Thomas Woodin.

St. Philip's Steeple, from the western churchyard. The first wrought iron gates to the yard had strong reminders of man's frailty—including skull and crossbones, which were replaced by more conventional decorations that date from the 18th century.

St. Philip's steeple and St. Michael's steeple dominate the skyline of the old city.

Viewed from this vantage point, the unusual use of three porticos on the church edifice is apparent.

146 Church Street. St. Philip's Church. Although this is the oldest Protestant Episcopal congregation in South Carolina, the building dates from 1838. The first St. Philip's was a small wooden structure on the site of the present St. Michael's.

William Rhett, nemesis of the pirates, presented the congregation with communion silver that is still in use. The building was badly damaged during the War Between the States.

Church Street traffic bends around the St. Philip's portico that juts beyond the sidewalk.

350 Meeting Street. Joseph Manigault House. Gabriel Manigault designed this Adam style house for his brother about 1803. One of the best examples of his work, it was offered for sale for non-payment of taxes in 1933. It was purchased by Princess Pignatelli as an early preservation effort and given to the Charleston Museum.

The form is that of a parallelogram, with bows on the north and east sides, and a bowed piazza on the west. A lovely circular stair, fitted into the north bow, rises from a wide central hallway.

The house has been furnished in impeccable fashion. Open to the public.

The drawing room of the Joseph Manigault house is furnished, like other rooms in the mansion, with period furniture. The set of chairs and sofa, with painted scenes, reputedly was used by Thomas Pinckney when he served at the Court of St. James from 1792 to 1796.

The portrait is of Elizabeth Wragg Manigault, painted in 1757 by Charleston's "court painter" Jeremiah Theus.

An upper story view of the gate house entrance to the grounds of Joseph Manigault house. The garden site was occupied by a service station before it was rescued and restored on the original plan; luckily, a drawing of the garden had been made before it was destroyed.

The only other gate house in the city is the massive one at the College of Charleston.

Rice grown in the low country brought wealth to planters and to Charleston, and it was honored in decorative pieces. Here, a bedpost of a valuable "rice bed" in the Joseph Manigault house.

116 Broad Street. Rutledge House. A 19th century architect made many changes in the facade of this house which dates prior to the Revolution. The magnificent wrought iron by Christopher Werner, one of the most gifted of all Charleston ironworkers, was added, as were the window cornices. This was the home of John Rutledge, for a time "president" of the ;independent ɨrepublic of South Carolina, governor of the state, a state chief justice and congressman.

39 Church Street. Eveleigh House. George Eveleigh, a fur trader, built this Georgian house in 1743. Though it was damaged by a hurricane nine years later and lost its roof in an 1811 tornado, little damage was suffered by the interior, which remains almost unchanged.

135 Church Street. Dock Street Theatre. The home of the Footlight Players of Charleston, this attractive building is on the same land occupied by a theatre that was erected in 1736. Later, it was the site of the famous Planter's Hotel which fell into ruins following the War Between the States. The present reconstructed building is owned by the city and was opened in 1937 with a production by the community theatre group.

A great deal of the material from the Planter's Hotel is incorporated in the reconstruction.

14 Legare Street. "Pineapple Gates". The finials are actually pine cones carved by nineteenth-century Italian stonemasons—in response to the owner's request for live oak acorns!

70 Tradd Street. There are many family heirlooms in this dining room of a private residence. The corner cupboard holds china which once belonged to Arthur Middleton. The portrait is of Humphrey Courtney, shown holding the bill of lading for perhaps the first cotton shipped from Charles Town.

54 Queen Street. Thomas Elfe House. This miniature single house once was owned by Charleston's most renowned cabinetmaker, Thomas Elfe. Because of the many fine details, it is believed he may have built the house.

The house has remarkably fine proportions and is unique among 18th century buildings. The chair rail is three inches lower than normal—making the ceilings appear higher. The cypress woodwork is comparable to fine furniture.

58 Church Street. The glory of azaleas surrounding a small reflecting pool and a planting of newly-green boxwood.

59 Church Street. A privately owned house, built about 1735, is a
showplace of eighteenth century pieces of varied background. The
magnificent needlepoint is original. On the left wall is an eighteenth-
century Adam style commode in satinwood.

59 Meeting Street. Branford-Horry House and garden in spring. Passersby can see this lovely informal garden through the porthole-like opening in the gate. The house is pre-Revolutionary, the portico a later addition.

54 Hasell Street. William Rhett House. The oldest house extant in Charleston, this home was completed about 1712 by the doughty colonel who led a party to capture the pirate Stede Bonnet and his men. The entrance stairs and piazzas are later additions.

This house narrowly escaped two major fires that took many pre-Revolutionary buildings.

When Charleston was a walled city, an avenue of trees led to the North Gate from this plantation house.

18 Bull Street. Blacklock House. Distinguished workmanship abounds in this fine double house of Carolina brick. The English red rubbed brick used in the arches are fitted with such skill that the joints are almost paper thin.

William Blacklock, one of the many residents who acquired wealth during an era of commercial expansion, completed this residence in 1800. Among his prominent contemporaries were Nathaniel Russell and Joseph Manigault.

53 Meeting Street. First (Scots) Presbyterian Church, with its prominent steeples, is shown in this view taken from St. Michael's steeple. The church was organized in 1731 by twelve Scottish families; the first building was erected in 1734. This building is the fifth oldest church edifice in the city. It was damaged by the hurricane of 1885, the earthquake of 1886, a tornado in 1938 and a fire in 1945. The burning bush (copied from the Seal of the Church of Scotland) is in the window over the main doorway.

Flower Vendors. In earlier days, hucksters musically chanted their merchandise as they led horse-drawn wagons through the streets, a custom that survives only in the selling of flowers on street corners.

8 Archdale Street. Unitarian Church. Home of the oldest Unitarian congregation in the South, this building was near completion at the outbreak of the Revolution. Part of the Independent Church of Charleston, it broke away from that church in 1817 and became a Unitarian Church in 1837.

Extensively remodeled and enlarged in 1852-54, the interior is modeled after the Henry VII Chapel in Westminster Abbey.

188 Meeting Street. Market Hall. Though somewhat overwhelming when viewed close-up, the stately proportions of this building become obvious and impressive from a distance. Designed by E. B. White, it is now the headquarters of the Charleston Chapter of the Daughters of the Confederacy. A second-floor museum is open to the public.

The ground floor contains shops. This is one of the few remaining 19th century market complexes in the country.

66 George Street. College of Charleston. The first municipal college in the country, this institution was chartered in 1786. The main building, designed by William Strickland, dates from 1828, but the portico and wings were added in 1850 by E. B. White, who also designed the porter's lodge.

136 Church Street. Huguenot Church. E. B. White designed this neo-Gothic edifice that dates from 1844, the third Huguenot Church to occupy the same site. The first was built about 1681. In Colonial times, services were scheduled so that planters could travel in large canoes to and from their Cooper River plantations with the tides.

6 Chalmers Street. Old Slave
Mart. The small central building,
which was built by Thomas Ryan
and his partner about 1853, was
used for public and private
auctions of lands, carriages, horses,
furniture and ships' cargoes—
including slaves. The building was
opened as a museum in 1938; an
exhibit of crafts that were taught to
slaves is on display.

Even such primitive paving as
cobblestones, now relaid in
cement, was not known until after
the Revolution. Ladies wore clogs
to escape the mud and even
horses had a sort of clog on their
hooves.

34 Meeting Street. Huger House and Garden. A shade-dappled lawn lends a sense of spaciousness and serenity to this garden in azalea season. The house, built in 1760, was occupied by Lord William Campbell, the last of the Royal Governors of South Carolina.

42 State Street. A towering
Magnolia grandiflora against a
brick wall (left background)
dominates this informal garden
that also features a small
reflecting pool. Another tree
that thrives in the Southern
sun is the crepe myrtle (right
foreground). Camellias in full
bloom are proof that the
picture was taken in early
spring; Charleston's semi-
tropical climate allows winter
only a short stay.
The urns were at one time on
the Exchange Building.

100 Tradd Street. This view of the cloistered garden is framed by a live oak and plantings of native bamboo. Early roses are coming into bloom. Designed by Loutrel W. Briggs, whose book, *Charleston Gardens*, is a definitive study of the city's gardens and horticultural history.

West Point Rice Mill, shown from across the Municipal Yacht Basin. Now used for offices, this is one of two rice mills left standing. In the years when rice culture was at it height, this was one of the busiest places in Charleston.

Charlestowne Landing. A facsimile of a trading ketch used in the period when
settlers were being brought, under the Lords Proprietors, to establish a city in the
New World. The first settlement began in 1670 when three small ships arrived here
on the banks of the Ashley River.

Now an historic park site, Charlestowne Landing is open to the public on a fee
basis.

Route 61. Drayton Hall. This magnificent Palladian house is under the aegis of the National Trust for Historic Preservation. Since none of the original construction has been disturbed by installation of 19th or 20th century improvements, the former Low Country plantation house is a treasure not only for its beauty but its authenticity.

Every room in the house is paneled from floor to ceiling. The single most striking exterior feature is the portico with Doric and Ionic columns of Portland stone that was imported from England.

Route 61. Magnolia Gardens. One of the show place gardens of the world; there are over 1,000 varieties of camellias planted on these extensive grounds. Originally called Magnolia on the Ashley, because of the long line of magnolia trees that led from the river to the house, the land was first owned and developed by the Drayton family.

Open to the public, on a fee basis, in the spring.

Route 61. Middleton Place. It was here that Andre Michaux introduced the first camellias to the United States in the 18th century; several of his original plantings remain. The oldest landscaped garden in this country, it was part of the rice plantation of the Middleton family.

Following the Civil War, when the house was burned, the gardens were neglected. But one hundred and ten acres are on the Register of National Historic Landmarks and have been rescued from overgrowth and returned to their former grandeur. The gardens, house and stableyards are open to the public for a fee, year round.

—*Photo courtesy Middleton Place.*

Route 52. Cypress Gardens, once a fresh-water reserve for a rice plantation. Visitors to these gardens may be taken in boats over the cypress-darkened waters. There also are meandering paths, bordered by heavy plantings of azaleas.

Now owned by the city of Charleston, the gardens are open in the spring for a fee.

–Photo courtesy South Carolina Department of Parks, Recreation and Tourism

A late afternoon stroll along the Battery—a traditional rite among Charlestonians.

Design by Richard Stinely